Western Novels by G. R. Howe

Dragons of Fire

Crow Woman on Deadman

Short Stories Out Of Kane

No Time To Trust

G. R. Howe

ACKNOWLEDGMENTS

I would like to thank the following people who took their valuable time to read and edit the manuscript. Their comments and suggestions were invaluable. Thanks especially to my chief critic and grammarian, Joy Howe, who has lived with every word. Special thanks as well to Vicky Clarke, Martha Howe, Rachel Montgomery, Jack Scranton, Pam Zeller, Von Zeller, April Christensen, Glenn Halsey, and Diane Halsey.

FOR JOY

PREFACE

There would come a time when he'd find himself sitting on the last pew of a white church on a Sunday morning. He'd sit there simply because he'd never sat there before and he would wonder about it, thinking he'd give it a try and see if it was any good. At that future time he'd be able to say that he'd known some decent, church--going folks. Not bad folks, just ordinary people. And by the same token, he'd known some other Sunday--go--to--meeting people who could peel the paint right off the wall just by the parting of their lips, who would rob a man blind if he wasn't watching.

At that future time he would never have been in a church, not as far as he could recollect. He would not think himself out of place, sitting on a pew, one worn boot resting on a knee, his sheepskin coat open to a faded blue shirt, and smelling of purple sage, timothy hay and tall pine. He'd admire the finery of the women sitting in the front pews for all to see. Whispers would reach his ears but he'd never think they were about him. That thought would never even cross his mind. The God he'd come to know had never been too concerned about where he sat on a Sunday morning, the wood smoke smell of his clothing, or whether his boots were worn down at the heel.

At that future time, wrapped in the fresh glow of an early spring, the fellow up front would wear a black gown; he'd stand up and preach hot fire and black hell, and talk about places Joe'd never been to and then, having heard about them, wouldn't want to visit. Eight minutes later, having heard enough, he'd stand up and walk out the front door, the jingle bobs on his spurs announcing his exit to all who'd care to listen. Every soul would turn in their seat. The preacher would stop talking. Silence would hang heavy in the room like an old winter coat in a hall closet. Outside, he'd stand and admire the distant blue mountains, their white tops jutting above low hanging clouds. He'd stretch his arms in the morning sun and determine it was best for him to get as far away from that preacher's hell as he could. It would be the last time he'd be in a white church with its picket fence and cedar post hitching rails. He wouldn't figure he'd be missing much.

In this present time, far away from white churches and picket fences, he woke up to pitch black darkness, a ringing in his ears that would not go away, and warm blood running down the side of his nose in what felt like a hot steady stream. He thought maybe he was dead, that he'd woken up in hell itself.

CHAPTER 1

He was a limp body: a body that lay where
it had fallen two days ago. All about him in
the warm air and the damp earth beat the
steady rhythm of life. There were living
things: a teetering stinkbug walking in
widening circles, a hungry woodtick posed to
leap on any passerby, a belly-shrunken
mosquito looking for blood. In that short time
they evolved, some passing through death,
some beginning anew. But not him. Not now.
Not yet.

This body had a very interested audience.
After he'd fallen magpies had been the first to
arrive, gliding silently on black wings with
white flickering chevrons. At first there was
one, then two, then six, then eleven. That was
the beginning. Later a pair of crows arrived
and drove the magpies away, but not far.
Their numbers increased.

Soon flocks of both crows and magpies roosted
in the nearby cottonwood trees watching,
waiting for the last flutter of an eyelid, the last
twitch of a finger. They counted the time,

waiting for that final second when there was no interruption in the cycle of life and death and nothing would be left but rotting, decaying flesh. It was then that they would consume his flesh in a frenzy of feeding.

The body lay in a clearing surrounded by old cottonwood trees. Over the rise and below him a creek ran amid a string of grey boulders and giant trees whose rings exceeded three hundred. Their dark spidery trunks reached ever skyward. On the higher ground above him, across an older, dry creek bed were the brothers of those trees. In a long ago spring cottonwood seed had floated on the air, blown everywhere, lifted by the breeze. It had caught hold of life in the damp earth left by the spring thaw. Later the fragile seedlings were watered by the dark thunderclouds of summer. Those giants now stood watch with the magpies and the crows.

At the base of the closest cottonwood tree, camouflaged by the trees' grey alligatored trunks, lay seven coyotes, all panting, red tongues lolling in and out of their grey cheeks in the dry July heat. They, too, watched and waited. Coyotes content in their impatience, waited until there would be no doubt, when, at the last, only white bones would remain to be carried away, bones to be gnawed come an early morning when their stomachs were aching for the stringy taste of grey rabbit and kangaroo rat and none could be found.

The crows and magpies argued amongst themselves like three year old children, overflowing with words about this and that and nothing at all. The larger birds, the vultures, had not yet graced this scene with their presence. High overhead they drifted in lazy circles. It was clear that they had thought about the body and were thinking about it still. Indeed this body was on their immediate agendas, the only entree on short menus written in dried blood and soon to be rotting flesh.

The man's crumpled body must have looked appetizing and smelled wonderful to these flesh eaters. The hair above his hat line was matted with dried blood and layered with fresh blood that had oozed and run across his cheekbone and around his ear, falling onto the red earth. A dark line ran midway down his temple. Another moved in a straight line behind his left ear until it disappeared into what once had been dishwater brown hair. It was brown no more, dyed dark by endless drips and drops of blood.

Small flecks of white bone decorated the edges of the wound like too much salt on dark meat. A lead slug had torn along the scalp a quarter of an inch into what was three-eighths inch bone. It had torn the skin like the straight edge of a razor, leaving a scalpel-like wound that cleaved the skin, leaving the glaring white skull exposed to the heat of the overhead sun.

Lying prone the man existed in an unconscious stupor. Unless you were a hungry crow it was difficult, if not impossible, to tell he was alive. There was no rise and fall in the chest, no puffs of dust from the nose where it lay pushed into the earth like a wedge of dried, yellow cheese. The blood had stopped running on the first day, twenty-four hours after the crows had run the magpies into the branches of the Cottonwoods. Already the flies had laid their eggs in the dead flesh placing them among the white flecks of bone along the edges of the torn skin. The eggs were enlarged and swollen. Soon they would be wiggling, crawling maggots fighting for space in the dead and dying flesh.

Life, as the man would come to know it, came slowly. He was pushed to the edge of consciousness by an empty stomach and a dry thirst that choked his belly and seared his lungs. It was further complicated by an aching, throbbing skull from which he could find no escape.

His awakening was tripped by a large raven walking up and down his pant leg, muttering about the incomparable injustices suffered in its life. It stopped to shine its beak on the under feathers of its wing, then to preen, then to watch with cocked head the warm meat that would soon fill its empty stomach. The bird was impatient. Squawking softly, it hopped over and across the waist belts, waddling up the arm then down to the exposed neck. Pausing, it glanced about as if expecting to be knocked away; then it seized the ear lobe in its beak and commenced pulling.

It wasn't as if the body sprang to life shocked by the thought of becoming dinner for a flock of crows. No, the "springing" was barely a groan, a wisp of breath, a whimper drawn across the washboard of pain that was his head. These signs of life were so negligible that the crow did not release its grip on the blood-stained earlobe. Instead it became more aggressive, bracing itself for a stronger tug. The body experienced the mental image of an elderly, grey-haired woman yanking his ear and shouting something completely unintelligible at him. It was the crow's latter attempt that brought a small movement from the hand and arm, a futile brushing away of an imagined mosquito. That small twitch startled the raven. It fled, hit the ground, a feather flying, then hopped into the air and glided to the lower limb of the cottonwood. The birds were quiet now, cocking their heads, watching, waiting, uncertain as to what was to come. The hand twitched again, a mere movement of a finger, and the thought of dinner evaporated from the brainpans of some fifty birds, fading like a wisp of grey smoke in the dry south wind.

There was more going on with this body than yanked earlobes and the swatting of imagined mosquitoes. This mind raced out of control in no discernable direction. The eyeballs danced rapidly behind closed lids. Then they stopped, seeing dark shadows diminished slightly by a partial moon hanging in the clouds of night. They focused not on a man sprawled on the earth but a boy fleeing in the dark in another time and place.

The boy ran. He smelled the dank smell of riverbank and bog, heard the unrelenting song of bullfrog and cricket, felt leaf and willow whip at his face. The legs were those of a nine year old, struggling to keep up, to catch up. It was dark. He was alone. Ahead of him he could hear the diminishing sound of horses moving steadily away from him. He ran harder, ran until his lungs felt like they were going to burst, ran until he felt he could run no more. Even then at that time, when who he was wasn't yet developed, he did not stop. Instead he continued to run, fearful of being left behind, fearful of catching up, fearful because his father had told him not to do what he was doing.

"Go hide," he'd said to him. "Do not follow me. Hear? Get to the trees back of the house. No. It would be better to hide in the cane

fields. *Just get out of here. Hide.*" His father had stopped talking.

"*Boy? What are you doing here?*" he'd asked. "*I really need you to follow my instructions. I need you to listen and do what I told you.*"

That being said, his father had knelt in front of the trembling boy seeming to memorize the boy's face. Suddenly he clasped him to his breast, hugging him until it hurt to breathe. Abruptly he pushed him away, seizing his shoulders in his two large hands. His father had glanced about then, his gaze returning to his son.

"*Boy,*" he said, whispering in the dark shadows of the lean-to, the moon a small glow in the east far across the river, "*you might have to be brave, boy. Braver then ever. If I don't come back...,*" He'd stumbled over the thought as if he didn't want to consider it, as if he deliberately pushed it aside.

"*You'll need to take care of your mother, your brother, your sister.*" The man paused. "*They'll be depending on you. You'll have to be a man.*" He stopped talking, pausing, as if thinking he was asking too much, the impossible.

Then he reconsidered. "*Don't worry about it, boy. Just do the best you can. Now get. Go on. They'll be coming. Get the hell out of here. I don't want them seeing you. I don't want you here.*"

The boy had run then, run around the edge of the house. He'd looked back at his father, saw him wave him on. Obediently he turned toward the cane fields, but he didn't go far, just far enough to be out of sight. Then he turned and made his way back behind the house.

He didn't think his father saw him after that for he was careful, waiting in the long shadows cast by a newly risen moon, hiding in the tall grass of the paddock where fences ended and the thick undergrowth began. It was there that brush became trees and trees became even bigger trees, where the great horned owl hunted river rats with impunity, and where the copperhead lived in silence. He didn't wait long for they came as his father had said they would--six big men on big horses, the last rider leading a seventh. They stopped in the packed front yard of the long white house. He saw his father step out of the shadows of the lean-to.

"I'm here." His father's voice was clear, carrying easily on the damp night air.

The riders, their features hidden from sight, turned as a group to the voice. The boy heard his father say "No." To what, he couldn't hear. He saw him mount the extra horse and watched as they rode off in the direction from which the riders had come. That's when he started running, trying to follow, trying to keep up.

That was then. This was now.

It was another ten minutes before the body moved again: the eyelids flipping open, seeing an ant crawling up a stem of prairie grass, moving up, then down, its antenna waving rapidly in the heated air. It was hours before he managed to sit up and stare at his new world through stricken, bloodshot eyes. There he sat, rocking back and forth, his body trembling, steadied against toppling over by his arms, conscious only of an aching, throbbing head atop his shoulders. What he saw didn't register; if anything it frightened him because it was unfamiliar. He recognized nothing.

The land fell gently away. Below him a line of cottonwoods followed a stream of water until it was lost in the haze, going somewhere beyond. In the distance, away from the stream, the land was brown, the color of dried grass. It was the grass of late July that perfumed the air and sheltered the grasshoppers. But he didn't know that, not yet.

In the shade of the cottonwoods an animal stood not a hundred yards from him. But he didn't know that either. He could only blink his eyes against the brightness of the midmorning sun and stare, rocking slowly back and forth, waiting for something to catch up with something else, for something in his brain to connect, to come together in rational thought.

Later he stood with difficulty. At first he tried unsuccessfully to get his long, skinny legs under him. Finally it happened, a motor response that at the time he neither thought about, considered, nor understood. There in the baking summer heat, in dried grass up to his knees, tottering as if an old man, he stood examining himself, trying to get a grip on what he was. He noted his pants: dark grey, worn and threadbare about the pockets, the bottoms of the legs tucked inside faded black, stitched boots. Those dusty boots sheltered his toes. He noted the underslung heels and spurs with Mexican rowels and jingle bobs. Dried blood stained portions of his "patched at the pocket" shirt, mostly on his right side. He wore a pistol belt that clung to his waist. The leather was oiled, stained dark brown, stretched from long use and the weight of a pistol. The holster was secured to his right thigh by a leather lace.

Standing was one task but walking another. In the beginning he staggered, catching his wobbly balance before falling to his knees only to stand up and fall again, again, and again. Finally, swimming in nausea, he sat on a busted log and stayed there, bent over himself, watching blood drops pile up in small puddles at his feet.

He made no further attempts to move from the log until evening. Under the relentless rays of the afternoon sun it occurred to him that he didn't know where he was going for the effort, or, for that matter, where he'd been, or even who he was.

In that heat he managed a decision. It was the first of which he was cognizant. He decided he wanted water, that he wanted shade, and finally that he wanted the ache behind his eyes to go away. Water was running amid the trees. Somehow in the mess that was his head he knew that. It was evening before he found it, or rather, fell into it and nearly drowned. In spite of himself he got some of it inside. There was strength in water. He immediately felt it, liking what he felt: the coolness of it, the soothing of his throat, the way it sat in his stomach. After a bit he drank his fill, crawled out of the mud and promptly succumbed to fatigue. No sooner had he closed his eyes against the reality of dripping blood and the searing headache than he found himself in another place, running.

He was out of breath. He ran, his slender legs churning, his face stinging from nettle, from vines that whipped across it, from branches that hung too low and sought to bar his head-long plunge. Eastward he ran, moving toward the dark river. The moon was sporadically blacked out by the spidery branches of tall trees. Far ahead he could hear the horses move through the night. He ran toward the sound until the sound stopped. The silence frightened him. Moments later he reached the edge of a clearing and stopped.

A half mile away from him a mass of horse flesh, barely discernable in the pale moonlight, moved steadily away. They were halfway across an empty meadow, a half mile from where he stood fighting for breath. Farther away still, beyond the horses, was a dimly lit building. It was hard for him to tell how far it was; it seemed a long, long way.

Even then, as young as he was, he knew there was cause for hesitation. The open feel of the meadow made him uncomfortable. If anything were to get him it would be out there where he couldn't hide. After some thought he skirted the edge of the clearing, keeping to the undergrowth. He arrived at the settlement forty-five minutes later and found the seven horses in front of a merriment house. Down the street he could see a general store. It sat in the shadows, its windows barred and shuttered. In the back of his mind he thought he'd been there before. But he wasn't sure.

He circled the large, square structure twice, clinging to the shadows, hiding behind mulberry and currant bushes. Finally he entered through one of the two back doors. Inside he found no one. No one occupied the pantry. No one was in the kitchen. It was dark and difficult for him to see. From deep inside the building he could hear voices, indistinct murmurings, and then footsteps. Quickly he scurried down a hall and hid in a broom closet, nearly tipping over a bucket of water. Waiting, fearful of being caught, he held himself still, barely breathing. He listened until the footsteps receded. Carefully he crept out of his hiding place, then fled up a darkened staircase onto an enclosed balcony.

Holding his breath, he hid beneath a table. After assuring himself that he was alone, he peered around a table leg and through the balcony's wooden slats. A room spread out below him glowing yellow in the lamplight. Chairs and tables sat neatly in rows waiting for customers now asleep in their beds. There were no patrons, no customers and no merriment that night. From his hiding place he saw nine men. There were the six men who had taken his father, and two additional men, sitting at a table littered with a collection of dark brown bottles and blue green glasses.

Some of the bottles were empty, some partially full. There were ceramic ash trays on the tables in no particular order. The men sat staring at his father who mutely occupied the middle of the floor, standing, his hands clasped together in front of him.

"Thank you for coming, Matthew." The man who spoke sat at the table, leaning slightly back in his chair. He talked with his hands, a dead cigar between his fingers, waving it at his father like a king with a scepter.

"It's not as if I had a choice," his father replied.

"It doesn't matter, Matthew. You are here. We can talk now."

"There's nothing to talk about."

"Nothing?"

The room erupted in a clap of thunder. The boy grabbed his ears, saw men diving for cover and a smoking gun at the end of the fat man's hand.

"Nothing isn't what I wanted to hear, Matthew."

The sound reverberated in his ears. The boy heard his father exclaim, saw him grabbing his stomach. "You gut shot me, you sorry black bastard!"

"I did." And the fat man shot him again through the mouth. His father fell slowly backwards, awkwardly hitting the floor, his booted legs jerking, twitching in death. Blood began pooling around his head, his sightless eyes blank. In that moment the boy saw the men, saw them all, their faces imprinted in his memory like a fiery brand, indelibly seared into his memory. Eight. Eight men, eight faces in a barroom. He would never forget.

When he awoke his clothes were caked in mud, mostly dry, and his mind was blank except for the dream. Vivid as it had been, it, too, began to fade, then rushed back lying just behind his eyes like a gaping hole, crying at him, reaching for him.

The heavy pistol that clung to his thigh bothered him. He wasn't sure why. He tried to stop thinking about it, and he stopped thinking about it several times before he dozed and merciful sleep again found him. It removed him from the ache in his head, that throbbing pain that followed him like a shadow. Reluctant though he was, sleep engulfed him in another world, in another time. In that stupor he didn't care who he was or why he was there. Those questions could wait.

This sleep did not give him peace, nor rest, nor rejuvenation. In this thin darkness of sleep the mental images returned, plaguing him. Repeating visions haunted him. Mostly they were the same; sometimes though they were different, variations on a theme.

His father spoke to the fat man with the dangling watch chain, the black smokeless cigar. "There's nothing to talk about," he said.

"But there is." The big man was staring up at his father from his chair. There was ice in his voice. "You're not going to make this difficult, Matthew, are you? That wouldn't be too smart."

Hidden under the table in the balcony, the boy didn't move but he didn't want to hear any more, either. Already he'd heard it, or something like it, yet it was happening all over again right in front of him. He knew what was coming so he grabbed his ears and tried to will himself away from the place. Then he heard the first shot. And there they were again, eight men, eight faces. Eight. Six of them diving for cover, a fat man laughing, pointing with his cigar, a gun in his hand. A second with light red hair sat at the table, wordless.

The cool of morning awakened him. He was thankful for it. He lay gathering isolated thoughts, blending them together, blinking his eyes against the light. Finally he sat up and blood started to drip, falling into his shirt pocket. Drip after drip. He watched it as if from a distance, as if through the eyes of a small boy running through the dark forest.

His mind shifted. It occurred to him that he wasn't alone. He knew there was an animal nearby and, somehow, it was his. He tried to remember where he'd last seen it, where he'd gotten it, what it was for, and why he had to have it. His thoughts were disrupted by the sharp throbbing of his head. *Oh God*, he thought. Then, *Papa, where are you? Don't let them....*

He collapsed and mercifully passed from this world into one full of kindness, full of softness, full of fuzziness, one without hunger or thirst, without a hard, unyielding ground and an aching, throbbing skull. It was there he lay when the horse found him, breathed on him, blowing air against his skin, smelling him and shying away at the smell of blood, then sniffing at him again.

Before the haze of consciousness clouded his mind, before the ache that was his skull dulled his senses, when everything was clear and bright, he lay in his blankets and a woman, her light brown hair pulled back away from her face, sat on the bed beside him. She stroked his young cheeks, rubbed his temples, ran her fingers along his scalp and willed him awake, willed him into consciousness.

"Time to wake up," she whispered. 'Come. Wake up." Her low, sweet, soothing voice pushed him. It was good, very good. But he didn't want to wake.

No. Not yet, he thought. Not when everything was so pleasant.

Yet the woman's voice continued. It pushed and pushed until she shoved him across the barrier he did not wish to cross into throbbing, relentless pain. "We need to talk, son."

No. No. He didn't want to talk.

Startled, his eyes popped open. Above him stood the animal. Mentally he tried to separate the dream sleep reality from the painful reality of breathing. He wondered if he was really awake. Or was it a dream? But there stood a horse, the horse, his horse. He thanked God over and over again and then wondered who God was that he should thank him. He tried to consider the horse and got just as far as he had gotten with God. Confused, he turned to look for the woman. Her voice had been so real but she wasn't there. There was no sign of her. The horse was real. He turned his attention to it. It was better to fill his head with horse than to think of his father or of the pain that rocketed through his head.

It was easy looking at this horse. The man laid on his back and studied the animal, looked at every line of him. He found a remote pleasure in what he saw from cannon bone to hip, to shod hooves, to the ever switching tail. The horse was tall with four stockings, a blazed face, a bar S bar brand on the left shoulder, a deep chest, and an expensive saddle.

He wanted to get closer. Eventually he tried sitting up, then rising on wobbly legs. To his surprise the horse did not move at his approach. Nor did it shy away when he leaned on the smooth, hard leather of the saddle, rubbed the cantle and the shoulders with his finger tips, fondled the riata, the rifle stock.

It wasn't long before he discovered the saddle bags. He was surprised at what he found; there was hard white, flaky stuff–he thanked God for that··and wrapped in a soft brown cloth, another pistol, and yet another. He found cartridges, dried meat·jerky··he thanked God for that, too··and a letter, an envelope containing a note written in an even hand. It said "Please come quickly." He couldn't read who it was addressed to or who had signed it. Just the word 'Darling." *Who was "Darling?"* His desire to know was not satiated, for those parts, the informative ones, the ones he wanted, were smudged and worn. He asked himself, why did he have so many pistols? And who was God that he talked to him all of the time?

His head hurt so badly that he was forced to hold himself still. He didn't dare move even a little. Yet he had to move; he couldn't stand still.

In the saddlebags he found a knife, the folding kind. With it he cut a piece of jerky, gingerly putting it in his mouth. He was surprised at the knife, surprised at finding it. He should have known about it, a knife with an ivory inset on the wooden handle. Sure, he recognized it, didn't he? Sure he did, yes he knew about it, but what did he know? The memory was there so close, right on the edge of his thoughts. *Just wait,* he thought. *Just wait. It'll come. All of it. But, 'Darling?' What was that all about?* He damn well should know.

Fresh blood dripped onto his shirt pocket. *How'd that happen?* There it was. *Hell's Fire!*

He'd known that the folding knife...it had been in his pant's pocket. But when?

More blood. The head wound? That must have happened when he was riding the horse. *Must have been, had to have been.* He tried to recall it but could not. Nothing.

No. No. Just wait. Be patient. It'll come. The horse had come, hadn't he? And he'd brought that crusty white stuff, and the jerky; he knew it was jerky and the white crusty stuff, what was that? Yes. It'd come. Just wait. That's all he needed to do. He'd just have to wait.

Waiting proved to be enormously difficult.

CHAPTER 2

Sleep pulled at him. He fought with it, fought it hard, not wanting the boy stuck in his head, not again. The boy was too close, too real. Maybe if he just stayed awake his aching head would quit aching. Then he thought about the woman and didn't mind the thought of sleep, except that she didn't much like him sleeping. And now he didn't like it either. Somehow his father 's death was all his fault. Maybe he could have stopped it. He sat watching himself, the boy. He was there. But, no. No, he could have done nothing. *Just too small*, he thought. *Just too small.* His thoughts returned to the woman. At length sleep took him but it brought no relief.

"We need to talk."

But he didn't want to talk. The woman, much taller than he, was standing in the living room looking down on him. She was going to tell him what he already knew. He wanted to hold his hand up and say, "Stop, I don't want to hear this."

Behind the woman's skirts he could see a small girl playing on a couch, pulling on the red woolen hair of a blue doll with black button eyes. She walked it across the top of a wooden box onto her leg, then across the cushions and pillows. She was humming to herself, talking to the doll, her light brown hair bouncing on her shoulders.

"Son, what I have to tell you is hard. I will be straight up. Your father's dead. He died. He's not coming home." The woman started to weep, covered her eyes, buried her face in her hands. Then holding herself very still, she looked at him, wiping the tears from her eyes.

"We got to be brave," she said. "We got to get on with living. That's what we got to do."

He could see a boy, part of his face, looking at him from the kitchen door. The boy was younger than he.

"I want you to know now. I don't want you hearing it from someone else. Your father was killed gambling. In a gun fight. He was in a shootout over cards. We have lost everything to cards, even this house. If it weren't for Mr. Mitchell letting us stay here for as long as we want we'd be out on the street. I just have to sign some papers. That's what he said. Me, being a widow."

She started crying again. The girl was singing louder, hugging her doll, then swirling it around the wooden box, her skirts billowing. The woman turned to her.

"Hush, Irene." she said. "Please be quiet. Momma is having a hard time, Sweetheart. Just be quiet for a moment."

"What's wrong, Momma? Why are you sad?" The child asked.

"Oh, it's nothing, baby. Nothing at all. I'll be all right in a minute. Just go on playing with your dolly." The woman blew her nose on a wadded up handkerchief and looked at him through worried eyes. "It'll be all right, son. You'll see. It will be all right. I'll make it all right."

The tears in her eyes were not very convincing. She wasn't very convincing. "Now take your brother outside and gather the eggs for me. I'll make breakfast." She turned toward the kitchen. "Jedediah" she yelled, "come here. Go with your brother. You two get the eggs. I'll heat up the coffee. Make some griddle cakes. Come, Irene. You come with me, baby. Bring your dolly."

The boy walked outside wondering why his mother had lied to him. There were no cards. There was no gun fight. Then he thought that maybe she hadn't lied. Maybe she was only repeating what someone had told her. She hadn't been there. He'd been there. He knew.

"Son?" His mother was standing on the porch of a long white house. Irene was hanging onto her skirts, the doll in her left hand, dangling it, swinging it back and forth. He turned to her voice. "Where were you last

23

night?" Jedediah was standing by his side looking at their mother, waiting to gather eggs.

He awoke with a start, sending a shooting pain from his skull to the bottom of his feet. His right leg cramped until he wanted to scream. Now he was wide awake. Wasn't he? It was dark. What time he didn't know and didn't really care. What difference did it make? He didn't dare sleep. *Sleep. No. No,* he thought. *Sleep and "perchance to dream." No.* He was wide awake now, thankfully wide awake.

In the darkness he rubbed his thigh muscles. He soon hovered between consciousness and unconsciousness, lost where dreams are sometimes remembered and never understood. In those dreams he was lost in groans of pain and fear. To escape his demons he thrashed about in his blankets, mentally running from the street dogs, their teeth hovering inches from his throat, then nipping at his legs.

That's where he lived when his eyes were shut tight and his breathing was long and labored. He wondered if he was there now, thinking that perhaps he had two lives--one full of pain while he was awake, one full of pain while he slept. He slept fearful of waking; he awoke fearful of sleeping.

Always there was the river: big, slow, filled with the color of the silt that it carried mile after mile, dropping it on the sifting sand bars, picking it up again, changing color and location, moving south. People changed, never identifying themselves fully, the stages of their lives changing. But the river remained; it kept on moving, its heavy waters swirling deep and black in the darkness of night and grey in the light of day. He found he loved the river.

The older woman would come to shake him awake, never allowing him to sleep. She'd done it before. She would again. But he wanted sleep. Her hair was grey and her skin was wrinkled, an alligatored patchwork quilt of dark and light. Sometimes she was young and he was not so old, but her voice was always distinctively raspy, living deep in her throat like a troll hiding under a bridge. In the beginning he thought that she was his mother; then he knew it.

And there was another woman, a girl, young like him, only younger. The older woman called her Irene. He thought she was his sister; then he knew it. Sometimes Irene was a baby girl, sometimes fourteen, sometimes an older twenty. Sometimes he didn't know how old she was because she cried like a child, then like a married woman who'd lost her lover to the river. Behind her, hidden in her skirts, were two others, a boy and a girl. Like shy puppies, they peered out at him from around her legs.

"What's you a doin', boy?"

All ten years of him looked up from the glass display case at the man towering above him. He was immediately taken by the fringe waving from the sleeves of the man's leather coat, the ivory handled pistol tucked neatly into his waistband, the Bowie knife secured behind a scarred leather belt.

"You lookin' at them shootin' irons?"

The boy was as tall as the counter. No, he was taller, just tall enough to be looking down through the glass, looking at pistols, at hand guns.

"He's been in here lookin' too much. Just about every day," said the man behind the counter. The storekeeper, his grey apron hanging loosely about his skinny frame, spoke through a handle bar mustache that drooped around the edges of his lips, hiding his wide mouth, his yellow teeth. He asked the man with the buckskin britches what he wanted.

"Let's see," was the answer. "I'll be needin' supplies: ten pounds of flour, five pounds of sugar, a bait of tobacco, a pound of salt, five hundred rounds...." Abruptly, the buckskinned man knelt in front of the youngster, the long fringes bouncing, waving as he moved. In mid-sentence he turned to the boy.

"Boy? Boy, what you lookin' at shootin' irons for? Your old man know you're in here? Does he know you're lookin' at shootin' irons?"

"They killed him," the boy replied.

"Matthew? Matthew's dead? You're Matthew's boy, ain't ya?" The buckskin clad man stared at him intently through unblinking eyes.

The boy nodded, wondering how the man knew his father, then glanced down wistfully at the line of pistols lying on white cotton in the glass case. He studied them, knowing they were more expensive than anything, way beyond his reach, way beyond his mother's reach. Somehow, he thought, somehow he had to get one. But which one? Any one, he thought. It didn't matter, not for what he had in mind.

It would matter to his mother. She'd already told him what she thought of guns. She was a church-going woman. He knew how she felt about them. Reading and writing and attending church on Sundays were high on her to do list. Not guns. He'd told her nothing about his father. Nothing at all. Not that he'd really lied when she asked. "I was looking for Papa," was what he'd told her. "I didn't find him." That was a necessary lie. It was better than explaining.

"You see this killin'?"

The boy looked at the man, nodded again caught by two deep blue eyes, the smell of horse sweat, chewing tobacco, and sage. He noted a dark mole along the man's neck and the long black hair growing out of it. The voice was deep as if dragged from a dark well. Inside those eyes there was something that grabbed him. One look and the boy wanted to tell him anything and everything. He wanted to tell him about the eight faces, the fat man with the round stomach and the cigar pointing at his father, the smoking gun, the laughter, the watch chain bouncing on the fat man's stomach. For some reason it was hard for the boy to take his eyes off the mole and the black, curly hair.

The boy answered, "A fat man shot him. He never even had a gun or nothin'. He was just standing there."

"A fat man, you say?"

"Yes, sir. There was eight of them."

The storekeeper broke the spell. "Boy, you scoot, now. You're botherin'..."

But the man wearing fringe looked up at the storekeeper, shaking his head slowly then turning his attention back to the boy. "Naw, Brig. He ain't botherin' nothin'. This boy, he's fixin' to buy hisself one of them shootin' irons. He figures to even things up with a fat man. That fat man like cigars, boy? He got a gold watch?"

"Yes, sir."

The man behind the counter chuckled then stated the obvious. "That boy couldn't buy hisself half a lick on last year's rock candy." The skinny storekeeper was looking at the other. "Foster," he said to the fringe wearing man, "this isn't where you should be goin'.

He's just a boy. You fixin' to get him killed dead?"

The frontiersmen rose to his full height. "Ya got any, Brig?"

"Got any what?"

"Rock candy? This here boy, he's shoppin' fer a shootin' iron. Some of that sugar might help him think proper. Might help him consider his options most careful like."

"But... Foster? Lord, do you know what you're a doin'?"

The leathered hands of the frontiersman were on the showcase. He was leaning forward, the fringe no longer moving, his eyes fixed on the man wearing the apron.

"He won't be wantin' no year old neither. He'll be wantin' the best you got, Brig."

"For hell's sake, Foster. He ain't old enough. You're gonna get him killed. He couldn't shoot the hat off his head with a pistol in both hands lookin' in the mirror. Give it up. You're talkin' crazy."

The fringe was jiggling when the man smiled. "You're probably right, Brig. But this boy...he's on a righteous mission. I can see it in his eyes. 'Sides this here is Matthew's boy. I owe him." The frontiersman turned to the storekeeper, giving him his full attention. "You owe him, too. Brig, I say we give this boy of his a little friendly help. Maybe our help, instead of it killin' him, it'll keep him livin'."

The blue eyes turned back to the boy. "You got a brother name of Jedediah? A sis?"

The boy nodded.

"See, Brig. This here's Matthew's boy. And we're gonna help him. You and me. It's the least...I can do."

"It's his funeral, Foster. Is that the least you can do? His old man is already dead. I'd really rather not."

"Maybe. Maybe not." The frontiersman was looking at the boy as if he were sizing him up.

"Boy," he said, "which one of those irons you got an eye on?"

"I don't know. All's I can do is look. I don't have any money."

The frontiersman smacked his lips. "Your Ma still alive?

"Yes, sir."

"She know you're here?"

"No. She wouldn't like it much."

The storekeeper chuckled. He'd pushed a large piece of rock candy across the glass toward him, then crossing his arms, leaned back against the wall to watch. No one else was in the store. It was still early. Outside in the dusty street the wagon traffic was light.

. *"Brig, we'll be needin' somethin' light."*

"A Derringer?"

"Naw, no sleeve gun. A six shooter, but light."

"Light. Somethin' for a woman?"

"Yeah, somethin' for a woman. Somethin' Colonel Colt made for the fairer sex. Maybe a pocket revolver of some kind. What do you have that's not a hide away? No forty-five, mind ya. No forty-four. That'd be on the heavy side. Somethin' smaller. Somethin' small and light for a boy's grip."

"There's this." The storekeeper bent over and seemed to be staring into the case. He reached in and laid his hands on a small pistol. "Yeah, there's this," he said. "It's a smaller caliber. Good for small squirrels and pack rats, I'd imagine." He handed it to the man he called Foster. "Good enough to get this kid killed; I'm sure of that."

The pistol came alive in the frontiersman's hands as he rotated it about his index finger. The boy watched as he checked the cylinder for live rounds by rolling it on his sleeve then hefting it, balancing it in his large, callused hands. It was magical.

"It ain't much, Brig. Feels too light. But maybe it'll do. Maybe it will get this young pistolero started. Maybe it's just the ticket for the train." The frontiersman paused looking at the storekeeper. "This all you got? Got somethin' else?"

The storekeeper nodded. "In that caliber and that size? That's it. Foster, you really ought to rethink this," he said. "Foster? You listenin' to me? You ought to rethink this."

The frontiersman wasn't listening. Instead he was studying the lad. "Well, boy. This is what it is. Now listen. I am goin' to be tellin' you some things. I don't expect you'll remember it all. Not all at once. It takes a while to be a shooter. It has to become part of you. In the end it has to become you. Brig here, he's goin' to help you remember. So, not to worry. Ya listenin'?"

The boy nodded. Behind the frontiersman he could see the storekeeper shaking his head slowly, wordlessly.

"Brig, what caliber is this? Who made it?"

"I'm guessing a thirty-three or maybe a thirty-eight," the storekeeper responded. "I haven't looked at it. O'Brien brought it in. Belonged to his woman. It looks like a smaller version of a Colt but there ain't any marking except for a serial number. It could be a special of some sort. Might not be a Colt."

"Well, it ain't going to matter none. I don't want him shootin' it. I don't want this boy shootin' nothin' til he is strong enough to handle a man-sized pistol...somethin' a little heavier."

"That's all I got, 'lessin' you want a SAA Colt. Might be a little big for a boy. And they ain't cheap."

"No, not yet. Later," Foster said. He was still twirling the pistol, flipping it through his fingers, pulling the hammer back, releasing it, like he was introducing himself to a piece of iron he'd never met before. The introduction didn't last long. A breath later he was looking at the ten year old boy as if there was no one else in the room and he was studying a wood tick crawling on his neck.

"Boy, this is good. This is the right size for a growin' lad. Don't worry about the caliber. You'll never fire it. This is for learnin'," the frontiersman said with a smile. "Let's just take one thing at a time. All right? Ok. First, I don't want you aimin'. Just point where you are lookin' and squeeze the trigger. Now, you're goin' to be leavin' this here pistol in the safekeepin' of Ol' Brig. Every mornin' you're goin' to come in and practice. How old are you?"

"Ten."

"Good. It's goin' to take sixty months for you to learn to use this iron and its big brother. This is all about work. Over and over again work. For every day you miss practicin', that's another day added on the end; that's another day before you can claim this here weapon as your own. Until that last day it's mine. It's Brig's, here. You don't practice, you don't get the pistol. We readin' the same book?"

"Yes, sir."

"Good. So, first: when it comes to shootin', you squeeze the trigger. I want you to get an ol' sock, fill it full of sand and a thousand times a day, I want you to squeeze it like you were juicin' an ol' cow. Half with the right hand, *half with the left. Remember, squeeze the trigger. That's your first assignment. Squeeze and practice squeezin'.*

Number two: You gotta know how to bring the pistol to bear on the target. Ya gotta get it out before you go to banging away. Ya gotta get it out of the holster, out of your waistband, front and back, with either hand and then point it at something small, real small. If you're shootin' at a fly, aim for the left eye, lower half. That takes practice. This means you need to be here where Brig can see you. You'll jerk and fire, jerk and fire, again and again and again, with each hand. From every imaginable position. And I mean every position: on your back, on your belly, just standin'. And every day, every single day. Understand? At first, no cartridges. Later, after you have done all I'm askin' you to do, we'll do hot lead. Not 'til you learn. Gotta learn first. So, no cartridges 'til you're strong enough and practiced enough to hold the weapon steady on target.

"Third: you'll need to get strong. To get strong, I want you to do exercises. You'll need strong arms, strong hands, strong fingers. You'll need to lie face down on the floor and push yourself away from it with your hands and arms. Keep your feet together, your back straight. Do a hundred everyday as fast as you can. On your fingertips. Got it? Every single day for the next five years. Understand?

Every single day. If you can't hold a gun it don't make no difference whether you can fire one. You'd miss, anyways. Ya gotta have arm strength, leg strength, belly strength,. All of ya's got to be tough as rusty nails."

The boy nodded. He glanced at Brig and back at Foster. "Yes," he said aloud, not believing his ears, his absolute good fortune.

"Boy, this is goin' to be hard as all billy hell. Possibly the most difficult work ever. I do not know if you're up to it. So you can quit anytime you get tired and want to. Guns are dangerous. They ain't ta' be played with. They're necessary to protect yourself but they are just a tool, as good or bad as the man packin' 'em. They are a way to an end. In the hands of the wrong man they are bad, very, very bad. They kill good people like your pa and a thousand others.

"I'll teach you how to know when to use a firearm. It ain't, boy, anytime you get yourself all pissy. It ain't when you're angry. It is when you're hungry for venison. It is when someone is killin' your ma, your brother. It is when the fellow in front of you is fixin' to take your life." The frontiersman was on one knee. "I'll tell ya, Boy...in this here country you can't live as a man without knowin' and packin' a shootin' iron. It's just not possible."

"I don't have a choice?"

"Do you want one?"

"No. No," the boy said without a moment's hesitation, not really sure what he'd just asked.

"No, you don't," the man said. "Not really. And it is goin' to take five years to learn it from top to bottom. Not a day less. Bein' a boy, unless you do as I'm tellin' ya, you'll not be able to face and best a full grown, angry, fat man, or a drunk with a gun and a rottin' apple for a brain, showin' himself off or a bull buffalo comin' right at you doin' a hundred miles an hour, snortin' blue smoke. You simply will not be strong enough in your head or your arm. So given all that, ya ready, boy, to give your soul to the Devil?"

"Yes, sir."

"Good. I figured ya might be. Let's go out back and pretend we're shootin' the place all to hell. In the next hour I'm goin' to fill your head with gunsmoke and bullshit, boy."

The storekeeper was still shaking his head "no" but he didn't say anything. He watched them go out back, the silver pistol small in the frontiersman's hand. On the edge of the counter the rock candy sat where he had placed it, waiting for the boy's tongue. I'll be damned, the storekeeper thought, as he picked it up and plopped it in his mouth.

CHAPTER 3

In the early morning darkness he awoke to the endless headache and a crawling, itching sensation along his scalp, bubbling as if it was dancing all by itself. He dared not touch it because he couldn't see it and touching it might hurt even more. It throbbed so badly; the pain was so sharp. God only knew if he could stand any more. He sure didn't know.

But he did know that he was hungry. He dug out a piece of jerky and chewed it until it was soft enough to swallow. The trouble with chewing was that it was somehow connected to his head and even the chewing hurt.

It felt odd to him, maybe even ironic, but the ache in his stomach was tied somehow to the pistol strapped to his waist. Almost as an afterthought he flipped the strap from the hammer and pulled the pistol easily from the holster. What he saw filled him with horror. Dried mud clung to the grip, the cylinder face, the trigger guard. The pistol was covered in mud. He could hardly breathe; the sight of it left him shaking like an old, old man, water welling up in his eyes. It was that one straw too many, that one step too far. He collapsed amid the dry humus and tried to pull himself together, the pistol in his hand.

And so it was that he came to be perched on a flat rock, sitting in the warm sunlight, a breeze playing with his hair, a Colt 1872 SAA on his lap. He removed his shirt and used it as a cleaning rag. Carefully he disassembled the revolver, removing the cylinder and each cartridge, cleaning each part thoroughly. Carefully he reassembled the firearm, worked the action, thumbed the hammer back and pulled the trigger. There was a joy in listening to the click, in watching the cylinder rotate, in spinning the revolver in his hand when he was through. He thought this pistol was bigger than the boy's in his dream. Much bigger. Heavier. Better.

A sigh escaped through his chapped lips. With the pistol in his hand he felt safe. It had a smooth wooden grip, a seven and half inch barrel, .45 caliber cartridges and, though he didn't know it or remember it, someone had modified it, had removed a little iron here and there, had strengthened a spring. After all that, the trigger was a bit more sensitive, the action smoother, quicker, lighter.

"This is just a tool, boy. The difference between this Colt and a hand rake is that your life depends on it. Treat it, mother it, sleep

with it...be kind to it...like your life depends on it. Because it does, boy. It sure as hell does." Foster Smith was staring right at him, not blinking an eye, not wasting a word, holding him to that single truth. "Life is what it is, boy. Protect it cause the good Lord ain't givin' ya no second chance."

His head still hurt and his shoulder was a little sore as he sat on the rock and looked at the grasslands that stretched forever, clear to the far blue mountains.

"God may be a forgivin' soul, but there are two things God don't forgive." Foster Smith was looking at him, a small, small boy. Brigham Larson was looking over his shoulder, standing slightly behind Foster like a watch dog. "He don't forgive bein' slow and he just hates bein' stupid. So practice, boy and find yourself in school."

He brushed off the sleeves of his shirt, then put his arms through one at a time covering his bony shoulders. Finally he felt like he could breathe, even with a dirty, blood-stained shirt buttoned up to the last button on his collar.

An hour later, driven by hunger, he went hunting. He spotted a grey rabbit. The pistol came up, bucked in his hand as it roared in the morning air and in that instant the rabbit was dead, shot through the head. He hadn't thought about it. It had just happened, like taking a step, blowing a kiss, taking a sip of coffee on a cold, frosty morning. It had taken no thought, no real effort.

He skinned the rabbit, cooked it on a stick over a small fire and ate it, bone by bone. It needed salt and something else. Sage, maybe. Pepper. Afterwards he added the kill to the inventory of what he was. *It was something,* he thought. *Something more.* A little while longer, maybe tonight, maybe in the morning, and he'd be right with the world. He'd know who he was and who "Darling" was and why the recipient of the note needed to hurry. *To hurry for what?* He'd know, and soon. *Real soon,* he hoped. He still had no memory of how he got the head wound, or why. And he had little patience with waiting to find out. He was sure there was not much time for it. Frustrated, he waited because waiting was all he could do. He laid down, his stomach full, and rested on his blanket. Sleep did not come easily.

Brigham Larson, his arms folded, was leaning up against the fence watching the boy like a skinny rooster watches a slow grasshopper.

This ain't going to take all that much time, he told himself. That Foster was probably in the next county now. He'd better be. Larson knew this was going to happen. Foster had these ideas. Somehow he got stuck with them.

"Make it a rule, boy," Larson said. "Never pull that damn thing unless you mean to use it. Once you do, use it fast. Hesitate and you're dead. Understand me?"

"No."

"Good answer. Simple, really. You wave a pistol around and someone will shoot your fool head off thinkin' you are gonna kill them and they need to save themselves. If you do pull the iron, shoot because everybody else is goin' to be. Remember this, most folk do not want to get into a shootin'. They'll be scared. They have to build up to it. They'll talk a lot, be real boisterous. Some, they'll get drunk so they aren't thinkin', so they'll have courage. If it is gonna happen, just shoot. It's safer."

Brigham Larson stared down at the boy, shaking his head slowly, wondering what the hell he'd gotten himself into. Finally he unfolded his arms, ruffled the boy's hair, and sat down on a stump.

"Foster and I have a difference of opinion," he said. "We have several. Foster thinks you practice shootin' fast, using pure reaction. He thinks it's best. Personally, I like takin' my time, not missin' the first time. You'll have to figure that one out yourself. The way I see it, if you don't miss the first time, you won't need a second time. Foster likes to shoot the hell out of everythin' from the get go. He figures

that if you practice not missin', you won't miss. I suppose that if you don't rush your shot you'll be all right." He paused, then. "You tell your mother you're workin' for me?

"Yes, sir."

"You give her that two dollars?"

"Yes, sir. But why, sir? I really didn't do anything."

"Not the point, boy. Fact is, Foster and I owe your father. So we are givin' it to you to give to her. She don't need to know what we're doin' here. I'd just as soon you didn't tell her. Gives you a reason to be here. Foster seems to think you need a lot of gun learnin'. You been squeezin' that sand sock?"

"Yes, sir."

"I'll be damned. Doin' those arm exercises?"

"Yes, sir."

"Ever' day?"

"Yes, sir.

"Well, I'll be damned twice. All right. Let's get on with it. Today, we're goin' to start jerkin' that pop gun. We're gonna see if you know the difference in squeezin' and pullin'. See whether you got the knack or if you're gonna have to work. Now remember what I told you. The hammer is cocked as it is bein' drawn, not later. Doin' it later will get you killed. Once you open the dance, don't stop movin'. Everythin' will be goin' to hell around you. You keep movin' forward, to either side.

42

Shoot while you are movin'. I'll show you how to hold the trigger down and let it rip. But that's later.

"For now we'll do one shot at a time. And, boy, always keep loadin'. If there is a lull, load. If you're empty, load. I'll teach you how to have three fully loaded and ready; but always, at every opportunity, load and reload. I'm gettin' ahead of myself since we're not shootin' yet but I can't stress this enough. An unloaded iron is worthless. It will get you killed. Understand?"

"Did you say three?"

"I think carryin' three is best these days. Knew a man that carried six, one on either holster, one in his belt behind and in front, one under each arm. He had those heavy navy colts; took a while to load up so he carried six so he wouldn't run out. That was the late war, boy. Blue and Grey. When he sprang into action that was somethin' to see. Not too many men can fire away with either hand. And of those that can, most ain't too good at it. He worked at it all the time, both hands. Claimed that practice was damn good insurance. Foster, he thinks you need to use both hands. You squeezin' that sand sock with both hands?"

"Yes, sir."

"Well, I'll be damned. You sure are a cracker."

"Yes, sir."

Brig chuckled. "Let's get started. Too much talkin' wears me thin."
"Yes, sir."

He woke thinking about a sand sock, Foster Smith, and Brigham Larson, and remembering that every Saturday he took two dollars to his mother much to her continued amazement. Once each spring and once each fall Foster Smith tested him and when he was fourteen he bought him a beer. It tasted awful but he didn't say so. When he was fifteen Brigham Larson gave him twelve hundred dollars to give to his mother and told him he couldn't teach him anything more. He remembered that. He remembered Foster taking him to Rock Creek where they shot bottles until there weren't any more and then they shot parts of bottles until there were only parts of parts. They shot plug nickels, knot holes, circles on a piece of driftwood and poker chips flipped into the air. They shot on the ground rolling and standing still, moving to the right and to the left.

Foster had said to him, "Boy, you think you are good now but practice and you can get even better. You stop shootin' and you'll sure as hell get worse. Think, boy. You can always get another pistol, another shootin' iron. But you can't get another life. You only get one."

He was fifteen and he never saw Foster Smith again. He remembered that.

It was morning when he walked the sorrel upstream. Sometimes it was a waltz and other times a two-step. It was a dance but not to music. The horse walked and he, his hand around the saddle horn, walked with him. He stopped when the horse stopped and walked when the horse walked. He'd have ridden but he wasn't sure if he'd be able to get in the saddle. Thinking of riding made him uneasy, so he walked. It was slow going and aimless. The only direction was upstream. He saw another rabbit but he didn't kill it. He wasn't hungry for rabbit. He spooked up a four point buck, but that was a lot of eating and he wasn't that hungry. All of these things delighted him because he knew them and they were his because he knew them. Just seeing these animals made him a little bigger, added to what he was, gave him something to think about, to consider and reconsider.

Mostly he remembered Foster Smith and Brigham Larson: the smell of them, the feel of their hands on his shoulders as they explained the way things were and how they should be, the pat on the back when he did well, the scowl when they disapproved or, worse, when they thought he could do better and hadn't. He thought about his mother and frowned when he could not remember what she looked like.

Midday horse and man came across a small waterfall hidden in trees, sheltered in thick brush. He knew the place was safe, safe from something. *But what?* He pondered the thought but the "what" didn't come to mind. To hide, however, did seem like the thing to do. So he hid himself in the trees by the waterfall and the pond into which it fell. At first he thought time was his friend, but then he wasn't sure how much of a friend it was or if it was his friend at all.

He thought about the hiding. *Hiding is a good thing, but why is it a good thing? One hides, not to be discovered. One hides not to be found. One hides to be... safe. Safe from people seeking you. Seeking you to...do you harm. Harm. Harm me? But why?* He couldn't think of a single reason why.

As he stood leaning against the saddle horse, a new clarity gripped him, sending chills down his arms and spine. Someone was out to get him. That thought felt like it was something he should laugh at, but he did have a head wound. He could have been hit by a tree branch, fallen out of the saddle and hit his head on a rock. He could have missed the stirrup and been dragged by his horse. He tried to remember, tried to imagine just how it came about; but whether it was reality or imagination he wasn't sure. He'd been riding. *That was just logic,* he thought. *Pure logic.* It was a damn miracle he wasn't dead. *Was it that bad? I am most certainly not dead. Dead people do not have headaches and eat rabbit.* He chuckled to himself.

Still smiling, he loosened the cinch and pulled the saddle off the sorrel's back. Later he built a small fire and boiled some coffee. He was still chuckling when he pulled his clothes off and waded into the pool at the base of the waterfall. It was waist deep at the deepest part and it felt so good he laughed out loud. He looked down into the clear water and saw a maggot bobbing in the ripples. That stopped him. He shook his head and another fell into the water. The laugh became a halting giggle. *What a day! Now I have maggots eating my brain.*

He waded across the pool to the green, glistening rocks and sat down amid the tumbling water. What had his life come to? Water poured across his head and shoulders, dripped down his back, ran down his nose and face. The falls cascaded down, falling ten or eleven feet, bouncing off the moss covered rocks, sending a mist into the air. It wasn't much water, just enough to keep the pond full, to feed the creek that wandered away, the very one he'd followed.

The water wasn't cold. It ran far too slow and too far to be cold. It ran until it fell from the ledge above him, onto his head, onto his bare shoulders and on his maggot infested scalp. And there he sat, a wounded man. The cascading water beat open the wound and drove the wiggling white bastards out. They rolled down his chest into the pond of water, wiggling until they drowned, their puffy white bodies floating away.

Past caring, past being able to care even if he had wanted to, he perched amid the slippery, green rocks, lost in a shower of falling water, lost in the pain that ebbed and flowed through his bowed head. Without any effort he drifted in and out of consciousness, escaped the pain, avoided the torture of thinking about nothing because he could find nothing to think about. Slowly the tension that hid itself in the muscles of his shoulders, his neck, his back, dissipated under the relentless drumming of water, and he slept, his head resting on his knees.

For that moment nothing mattered. There were no voices muttering in the darkness, no unblinking eyes staring into the starless night, no unending longing for heavy footsteps on the porch, the squeak of the screen door, for an arm around his shoulders; there was nothing.

The woman came, scolding him, calling to him across a swirl of darkness. And there was someone else, a young male's voice; but he couldn't see the source. Then the voice faded back into the woman's voice and she called to him over and over again. He tried to listen, cocking his head first one way then another, but he couldn't hear what she was saying. The woman's arms were waving; her mouth opened; her lips moved, but nothing, no sound. No matter what he did, his ears heard nothing. It was just too far off.

Then suddenly he heard her, a clear voice, as though he was standing in the kitchen washing forks and wooden spoons and she was standing beside him.

Jed! Joseph! Babe! Supper! Come wash your hands. Clean yourselves up." The woman paused. "Where are you? Children? Your supper's getting cold. Get in here before I throw it to the dogs, the hogs, and the chickens.

"Where'd you get two dollars?" Her voice was lower, full of doubt, full of all sorts of suspicion. Three sets of eyes were on him, holding him to the kitchen chair like a twenty pound sack of flour.

"Mr. Larson, Mother."

"Why? I'm not needing no charity. Joseph, this is charity. I can see it plain."

"No, Ma'am. It's not. It's for a week's work. I worked for it."

"That's too much for a boy sweeping the floor in a general store. I won't have it." She slammed her fist into her open hand.

Silence hung over the greens and peas like water on wool in a Texas downpour. Somewhere in the exchange he had stopped squirming in the seat of the hardwood chair and stared at the angry woman that was his mother.

In the silence he said, "Mother," his words measured, "Papa's dead. We're alone. There ain't no one else. There's just us. I have a job at two dollars a week. If Mr. Larson will give me two dollars I am not giving it back. If you won't take it I'll give you what you will take. I'll keep the rest and I'll buy what we need."

His lip was trembling but there was no waver in his voice.

Again it was his tongue that broke the silence. "Mother, I spoke to Papa before, before....before he didn't come back. He said if he didn't come back I needed to take care of you. I'm doing that, Mother. That's what I'm doing."

For a moment his mother stared at him. She hesitated then collapsed in the wooden chair closest to her, buried her head in her hands, and wept. It was then Joseph glanced at his brother, his sister, and then at his plate. In a room silent except for the sobs of his mother, he started to eat. A coldness settled in his heart that had not been there before. Eat, he told himself. What else was there to do? This spinach could sure use some salt and...some pepper. Some butter would help, too. The black eyed peas were good...well, maybe a little butter would help. Eat, you'll need it, he thought, for the exercises you're going to do, for squeezing the sand sock. He *glanced up at his brother and sister. They were eating also. Not a word was spoken between them.*

He woke with a start. For a moment he couldn't remember where he was or how he got there. It was bewildering. He studied the faint reddish, blood-stained water, felt it dripping down his face and down his chest into the pink foam at his feet. For a moment he thought about the dream he'd just had, tried to tie it down, tried not to forget it. An awareness dawned as the mental images ebbed and flowed, some disappearing into the pink brine. He fought to hold them as if they were slippery wet rocks falling through his fingers. Suddenly they returned and he fastened them in his mind, set them where he could see them clearly.

He took a couple of breaths and stood, stepping carefully out of the cascading water and along the wet, green rocks. He waded across the pond to the shore, heading for his saddle, not that he was going anywhere. It is hard as hell to go someplace not knowing where you are. Instead he removed his bedroll and spread it out in the high, dry grass, fell onto it, and slept.

The pistol recoiled in his hands. In his mind he knew this was no woman's firearm. A Frontier SAA Colt, Army issue. The cords in his arms and fingers were tight against the recoil. The pistol in his right hand was pounding at the tin can, the first shot making a hole, then each shot thereafter making the hole larger. Before the first pistol was empty his left hand brought the second pistol, identical to the first, from behind his back. In a single motion, he replaced the first in the holster and took the third from his waistband, firing all the while, never losing his concentration. Eighteen shots-all inside the hole in the can. Behind him someone clapped.

Now the voice said, "Use both hands at the same time; first one, then the other, then both at the same time. Boy, do you want to take a break, first? You up to it?"

"I'm up to it, Mr. Larson."

And he was. He had been every day for the better part of four years.

CHAPTER 4

Twenty-six hours later he was wide awake staring into a blue azure sky. Immediately, fearful of forgetting, he reviewed what he could remember. Some things he could not remember. Those thoughts he did recall he kept in the forefront of his mind, trapped in his mind's eye so there was no escape.

The words of Mr. Smith and Mr. Larson kept coming to mind, over and over again. This time he heard them clearly: *"Get yourself up, boy, let's chisel ya down some, knock some of those edges off ya,"* and, *"Now don't you go quittin' on yourself ya hear,"* and, *"Quick ain't quick. It takes honin' and bonin' and groanin'. It takes day in and day out of pushin', tuggin', pullin' and just plain workin'."* His favorite: *"Damn it, boy, that ain't nearly as good as it could be. Do it again,"* was closely followed by: *"Practice don't make perfect boy, never has. It's perfect practice that get's ya there. Nothin' less."*

This involuntary review left him smiling at first, then aggravated because it replayed again and again. Always there was Foster

Smith grinning at him, and Brigham Larson just over Foster's shoulder, nodding his approval. *"You can do it, boy. Just shoulder the load and keep on movin'."* Brig always seemed to have the last word. He'd be rubbing his chin as if the week's beard was bothering him, then he'd say, *"There's just one other thing, Joseph..."*

Joseph?

He ate the last of his provisions and slipped back to sleep, awakening in the early morning to ravenous hunger, a dry cotton mouth, itching skin, and a feeling that someone, somewhere was watching him. *That woman,* he thought, *she is watching me.* It was morning and he tried to remember her and could not. He hated that. She was his mother. He ought to remember his mother. He ought to remember what she looked like. It was as if he was living two lives but they ran along separate paths, never crossing, never overlapping. *"Patience, boy. Ya ain't gettin' there today."* But when?

"Ah for hell's sake, boy. No one ever shot the eyes out of a rattlesnake the first day or even the hundred and fiftieth day of tryin'. You're goin' about this the wrong way. Now listen. Stop tryin' to be faster than you are. Fast will come. The problem with tryin' to be what you ain't is that it's causin' ya to make mistakes. That will get you dead. So slow

down. Do it right. Second, now remember this: To learn how to shoot the eyes out of old Mr. Rattler. Ya gotta learn to be Mr. Rattler. Ya gotta know he's gonna be at the gate before he knows he's goin' to the gate. You'll never shoot his eyes out until you know what he's gonna do, where he's gonna be, and how he's gonna get there. Ya gotta think, boy. Think."

The bloodied man burst out laughing. "Ya gotta think, boy. Think." The sorrel jumped and stared at him, his ears bent forward. "All right, Foster," he said, looking at the sorrel. "All right. I'll slow down. I'll stop pressing. I'll think." To show he meant it, he stood up, stretched, looked around himself. He forced himself to do it slowly, noting everything, from the scarred cottonwoods, to the deadfall that lay across the creek as it left the pond, to the blue lichen on the rocks above the waterfall.

Having done that he spread his blanket out on the ground and on the blanket he placed all of his possessions, including his saddle and saddle blanket. Everything. He emptied his saddle bags, the rifle boot, and his pockets until all he was and all he had lay in front of him.

Emptying his pockets made him smile for there was Foster Smith looking with him. *"Never judge a man by what he's got in his pockets. What he's got ain't what he is."*

"All right Foster, I'm not this but what am I?" Before him was a Winchester Rifle stamped New Havens Arm Co Model 1873. He ejected all of the 44·40 cartridges and reinserted them in the magazine. Next to the rifle lay a pocket knife and three pistols, each marked Colt's Pat. F.A. MFG. Co., Hartford Ct. They had walnut grips, and five .45 caliber center fired cartridges, each with hammer sitting on an empty chamber. There were five boxes of ammunition and a Bowie knife in a worn leather scabbard decorated with round silver tacks. The knife was so sharp he could shave the hairs off of his arm with it. He counted paper money totalling three hundred twenty·five dollars and two twenty dollar gold pieces. With the paper money was a folded piece of old paper with a "please hurry" message.

In addition there was one metal dinner plate with a fork and spoon. Beside it sat a small packet of salt, some black pepper, and something that looked like ground up chili peppers. Lastly, there was a thirty foot riata tied to the saddle and a sheepskin coat, canvas on the outside, with leather trim that protected the pockets and black wool for the collar. The latter had been tied to the back of his saddle on top of his saddle bags below his bedroll.

Removing the coat from the back of the saddle, he checked the pockets: two on the outside, one on the inside. One of the outside pockets contained a pair of soft leather gloves. The second one was empty. The inside pocket was stuffed. It contained a doll with red woolen hair, a blue body, blue legs, a white lacy dress, black button eyes, and a letter. The letter was addressed to a Mrs. Sarah Johnson, New Orleans. Inside the envelope was a letter folded around a second letter. The first read, "Mother, give this letter to Joseph as soon as you can, love Jedediah." He smiled. Jedediah didn't have a whole lot to say to his mother. He thought maybe he would have said a lot more.

The second letter read, "Joseph, I really need your help. Please come as soon as you are able. Love, Jedediah." Below the signature was a post script. It read: "You have a niece. She's absolutely adorable. See you soon."

"I'm Joseph," he said to himself. "I must be. And I have a brother. His name is Jedediah. I have a mother. Her name is Sarah. I have a niece and I don't know her name. I have some friends; their names are Foster and Brig. I am somebody. And you're right, Foster, I am not just what is in my pockets."

The trouble was that having a name was like being a bucket with nothing in it. It didn't tell him who he was, what he did, how he got there or why. He was an empty bucket called Joseph. He had a brother that needed his help but he didn't know where to find him or what he looked like. He had a letter addressed to a woman in New Orleans, Magnolia Parish, Louisiana. It said 'come help me'. It didn't tell him where. How would he know when he got there? Better yet, where was he right now?

Joseph was in a lighter mood when he went hunting. His head still hurt and there was a gnawing in his stomach but he didn't have any maggots eating his brain and he had a name. First he shot a jack rabbit and dressed it out on the spot. On his way back he shot a wild turkey and dressed it out as well. *There's no use in having innards lying about to draw flies.*

Back at camp he made a small, smokeless fire and roasted one then the other, seasoning them with salt, pepper and some dried chili pepper. The food was good and his hunger was gone. For the first time in what seemed like six days he felt like he was getting his wits about him. That was something; the irony being that he still knew a lot more about himself when he was sleeping and hardly anything when he was awake. *In time*, he thought, *it will change.*

There were no more maggots falling into his shirt pockets, no draining pus. All that remained was an itch that he dared not touch and then a sudden realization that he had no hat. The discovery shocked him. It was odd. He hadn't given a single thought to a hat, and now, suddenly, it was the only thought he could entertain. A spotty past and barely a present, all of that was comprehensible, even bearable. But being without a hat--that was inconceivable. He couldn't stop thinking about it, obsessing over it. He simply had to have his hat and right now.

Ignoring saddle, rifle and rope, without care of bridle or spurs, he strode to the sorrel horse, used the short picket rope and pulled a half hitch around its nose. Effortlessly he swung up on its bare back and rode off at a trot, pursuing his back trail, descending on yesterday like a magpie on robin's eggs. A beeline would not have been straighter. Like a madman he rode, searching his back trail. *How stupid*, he thought. *I haven't any idea where I am but I have to find my hat. As if a hat would solve my problems.* But he just couldn't stop thinking about it.

On the ground, hidden in the dry grass like a dime novel missing a page, he found a chapter of his life written in another language. The language: a scratch on the ground, a tuft of bent grass, a branch broken, a rock disturbed. He saw the spot where he'd been tossed from the saddle, where his body hit, rolled and laid. The hat, too, had rolled, then pushed by the wind had tumbled across the prairie grasses and had lodged in the bent branches of buck brush, greasewood, and sage.

It was revelatory discovering who he was and knowing in an instant who he was not.

The problem was it was just a hat. The problem was he didn't remember it. Nothing had changed. Yet, there it lay, wide brimmed, faded grey, with a high topped crown and a tarnished silver hatband. He picked it up, examined it, ran his fingers over the sweat stains and found a fresh crease where a leaden bullet had ripped. And in that instant he knew what had left him bereft of past, shallow of present, and feeling hostile like a wet rag feels wet. Trouble was the hat asked more questions than it answered.

Still there were some things that were settled. He hadn't fallen off his horse like some tenderfoot, some greenhorn fresh from the city. He hadn't been struck by lighting. He hadn't been dragged around with a boot caught in a stirrup or knocked loopy by a low hanging tree limb. He'd been shot. *And damn near killed!* He might not have any memory but the memories he had weren't bad. They were fresh. He chuckled, caught up the sorrel, swung up on its bare back and rode off to collect his saddle and his gear, somewhat relieved. The faded hat sat perched on his head cocked off to the side. He was alive. Some 'sumbitch' had missed him. Not by much, but enough to make all the difference. Shooting at him was a mistake, a bad, unforgivable mistake; one that he intended to correct. *The sumbitch.*

Little things add up. Small, inconsequential events--details--they are always part of a bigger puzzle. That's what Foster taught. That's what Larson insisted upon.

"Think, boy. Think. Pay attention to detail. Open your fool eyes. Actually see. Actually listen. Boy, ya think ol Brig is bein' hard on ya. No. He's not. He's sayin' that the best way to keep suckin' in and breathin' out is to just be aware. There ain't no secrets. Just look around ya.

"Boy, what's that water hole tellin' ya?" Foster Smith was talking casually. He'd been talking all morning, asking question after question, one right after another.

"I don't know, sir."

"Don't be lazy. Look! Listen! See any tracks around it?"

"No, sir."

"Why?"

Joseph thought. *"Sir? Could it be that it's a trap?"*

"It could be. Somethin' is keepin' everythin' away from it. Could be poison water. Could be somethin' hidin' in the brush waitin' for supper to show up. Could be someone waitin' for you. It should bust out the flags in your hea and send the bells a clangin'. It should scream at you. It's tellin' ya to take care. Take care. It should be causin' ya to

take a look before you step down to take a drink or let your horse drink."

Larson sat his horse looking out across the grass to a stand of trees. "Boy," he said, "what's those birds tellin' you?"

Joseph looked at the closest tree full of singing blackbirds.

"Mr. Larson, those are happy birds. There is probably nothing bad around that tree. Nothing that has moved. If they suddenly fly, maybe there is something. If they come back to the same tree, maybe nothing. But beware, anyway, because something could be holding itself still waiting...waiting for me or something. Best to always be on the safe side."

"Good boy. You're learnin'."

CHAPTER 5

The next morning, hat cocked off to the side of his head so as not to press too tightly against his healing wound, he rode in search of something more to tie himself to, something besides dreams and jerky and an old banged up hat. An hour later he left the cottonwood trees behind and found himself riding in quaking aspen and pine. Later he rode out of the timber into a shallow clearing and discovered the remains of an old wagon road.

Finding a road startled him. It gave him pause to think that he might not be entirely alone. It took a few minutes before he was willing to cross the road to the other side, noting first that to his left the road disappeared quickly into a pine forest. To his right, however, the pines thinned and he could see farther. That would be north. It occurred to him that he'd been riding west. He asked himself, *How do I know this? How do I know these things?* Perhaps the moss growing on the north sides of the tree trunks told him, perhaps the sun marching across the sky.

Perhaps he knew it because north was simply north.

Which way to go?

In this quandary he stepped down from the saddle, leaving the sorrel ground hitched while he walked up and then down the road a hundred yards either way. It was a road less traveled. Grass had grown up knee high amid the old wagon tracks, yet sometime in the last four weeks a light wagon, maybe a buckboard, had rolled along leaving a narrow trace of its passing, bending the grass flat against the earth in its northward journey. Long before, years maybe, the wagon traffic had been heavy, perhaps with freight wagons with wide iron rims. They had widened the roadway, grinding their tracks deep into the grass, compressing the soil, pushing it to the sides. Only deep ruts remained from their passing. But that was long ago.

In the end he chose to head north. Signs of the buckboard's passing intrigued him and gave him hope. He followed it.

The sun had crawled half way down the afternoon sky when he came upon grasslands that he named the Green Valley. The name wasn't especially creative. He named it "Green Valley" because that is what it was and because a mile down from the top of the ridge where he sat was a weathered barn. It sat like a fat toad in the afternoon sun. If it had ever been painted it wasn't lately. Weathered wood gave it a deep grey hue. The shake-shingled roof sagged a little on the south side but it was standing upright and in current use.

Beside it was a long cabin half hidden behind trees and bush. The parallel lines from its white plaster chinking made it seem longer than it was. Several other outbuildings stood below the barn beside some pole corrals that contained six head of horses. The corrals extended from the barn across a creek. A glance at the sun told him there should be smoke if anyone was thinking about eating supper come evening. There was no smoke from the either of the cabin's chimneys, one at each end. No one was cooking.

Patience, he thought. *Be patient. It could be a virtue here.* He waited an hour. Still there was no smoke from either chimney, no movement about the buildings. The corralled horses stood where they had been standing when he first spied them. Finally, he remounted and continued down the faint wagon road. He covered a mile quickly, encountering nothing that set off any internal alarms. He rode past the corrals. The horses could smell the sorrel, probably him, too. They looked a little hungry as they edged up against the poles, sniffing, shaking their heads at the flies, swishing their tails.

It was quiet, nothing out of the ordinary. Yet the quiet was unusual. The hair on the back of his neck began to stand up. He flipped the leather latch off the hammer of his holstered revolver, loosened the carbine in the scabbard. The sorrel slowed down, its ears cocked forward.

Where are the dogs? There should be dogs barking. They would have smelled him by now. The sorrel stopped, refusing to go any farther. In an instant the rider saw why.

In front of the sorrel and slightly to his left, lay a man, stretched out full length, lying in the middle of the hard packed yard as if he was sleeping. A couple of chickens picked the earth at his head but the man didn't move. A breeze parted his hair, whipping it around. Off to the side a felt hat lay resting on its flat crown.

No dogs, he thought. *Why's that?* To his right the barn doors creaked on greaseless hinges. An unearthly, thick quiet settled around him. *Obviously,* he thought, *the man is dead.* The earth was stained dark blood-red around his head. This death wasn't a natural death. The corpse was bloated pretty badly. *Must have been dead two, maybe three days. Maybe more, but not much. And in this heat, it didn't take long.*

He dismounted, checked his pistol as he did so, dropped the sorrel's reins, then approached the corpse. He glanced at the barn, the corrals on his right, the closed door to the house on his left. *Lord,* he thought. He might have even said it out loud.

A movement caught his attention. At the corner of the log cabin, barely clear of an overgrown lilac bush, stood a girl: blonde, four feet tall, who looked like she was six or seven. She wore a blue dress with small, faint red lines running up and down it, a faded red ribbon for a belt. No danger from her, but it didn't look good.

The dead man had been about his size, had his color of hair, and now had a hole between his eyes. *Rifle shot, maybe a Sharps*, he thought, *from some distance.*

The girl-child moved from the lilac bush, walked in a straight line toward him, and stopped. He touched his hat brim, nodded, and said "Ma'am."

"I ain't no ma'am," the child said. "I'm just a kid."

The rider nodded again. "Know this fellow?" he asked.

"Yes, that's my dad. He's been shot dead."

"Sorry."

"No need being sorry," she replied. "He's my dad, not yours, and besides, you didn't shoot him. You wouldn't be here if you did."

That sounded right, most likely was. Once the man was shot, the shooter wouldn't hang around. He wouldn't want to. How did he know that? He thought about it a bit and concluded that he didn't know how, but he knew it. It was just simple, ordinary, run of the mill logic.

"Your mother inside?"

"No. She's dead. Timber rattler. Got her on the neck. She was picking berries. I was five. I'm seven now."

Damn, she sure seems to be dealing with these tragedies—no tears, just facts. How's she do that? He knew he didn't know the answer, but he admired it, especially from a girl. *That Irene didn't hold a damn thing back.* Suddenly, he had his mother, his sister Irene, his brother Jedediah: each of their faces flashing inside his head, one after the other, slowly at first, then over and over. He shook his head to make it stop.

"Got anybody else?" he asked.

"No. I got you. That's it."

"Me?"

"Mister, there's you and there ain't nobody else. There's just me and there's just you."

The girl sort of choked when she said that. He didn't know what to do then, so he just stood there looking down at her, the mental images of his mother, sister and brother flashing through his mind.

"You got a name?" she asked.

Again, he stared at her thinking that he really ought to answer her question. After all he knew his name, or leastwise, he was fairly certain about it. No, he knew.

"Mister? People call you anything?"

Finally, he nodded his head but he said, "I don't know." He shouldn't have said that. He did know. *Joseph,* he thought. *I'm Joseph. I have a letter. It is addressed to me. I just can't read it. What's so hard about that?*

The child's voice was incredulous. "You don't know what you are called? Didn't your mom give you a name?"

Taking a breath he smiled, nodded his head again, then looked around at his horse. *What now? Why hesitate?* He turned to the girl, "I reckon my mother gave me one. It's Joseph. She called me Joseph."

"Joseph," she said, looking up at him, craning her neck. "You sure wear your hat funny, like it's falling off."

That brought a chuckle from him. "I do, don't I? Got myself rapped up the side of the head several days back. About a week, I'd say. And I don't remember much from before it. Sorta' knocked yesterday out of my head. Didn't do my today much good either. How about you? Do you have a name?"

"Millie."

"Ah, nice name, Millie."

"My mom, she named me that. I got a Aunt named Mildred so I got named Millie. I have a Aunt Irene. And I have a Grannie Johnson."

Joseph suddenly came up short. He could hardly breathe. "What's your Grannie's first name?" he asked already knowing the answer, anticipating it.

"Sarah."

This time Joseph did stop breathing. He turned to the body realizing that his brother lay dead not ten feet from where he stood. Anger choked him. He couldn't speak. He couldn't think.

"Joseph, are you all right?"

He nodded his head to the child.

She stared at him, "Joseph? I have an Uncle Joe. I really gots two. My Dad's brother and my Mom's brother. I'm loaded with a lot of Uncle Joe's. Joseph is a pretty big name, like in the Bible. It's fancy."

He smiled. "Well, Millie why don't you just call me Joe?" he said.

"Ok. Joe, do you cook pancakes?" she asked.

"Well, I don't know. Is it hard?"

"My Dad cooked pancakes, so I guess not."

"Your Dad?"

"Yes, I am pretty hungry."

"I guess we could give it a try." *Pancakes*, he said to himself, *do I cook pancakes?* "How long's it been since you've eaten, girl?"

She held up one, two, then three fingers. "Two or three days," she clarified.

"Well, Millie, let's see if we can put on the feed bag." All the time he was thinking, *Pancakes, do I do pancakes?*

It turned out that he did.

In the late afternoon Joe buried Millie's father. It took him three hours to dig the grave. Six feet is deep. Three feet is wide. It took another hour to carve a marker: Jedediah Johnson. Those two names he carved in a plank of wood with a screw driver as a chisel and a lead pipe as a hammer. It took a while because Millie was talking. He buried her father next to another grave. The granite headstone read: Abigail Johnson. There were no dates. A quart jar of wilted mountain flowers leaned against the marker. Cheat and wire grass had grown up over the grave and around the stone. The graves were not fenced in. They sat on a knoll overlooking the green valley, the barn, the house and the corrals.

He never thought he'd bury his own brother. He tried to fix his thoughts on Jedediah but he couldn't. They kept wandering until he realized that he didn't want to think about him. It was hard to imagine that he had a brother, that he was dead, that he didn't know him, that he couldn't remember anything about him.

Joe was bone-tired when he finished. To his surprise Millie was hungry again. He fixed her some bacon and cornbread because he wanted to and she told him that her dad had liked cornbread and bacon. Joe's cornbread, she said, was better than her Dad's. Joseph couldn't get her Dad out of his mind, asking himself over and over, *why?* It didn't take him long to tie his head wound to Jedediah's death. It sort of made sense to him. *Kill the Johnsons. Kill one, kill them both. But why?*

Yesterday, sitting back on the ridge waiting, Joe had planned to stay the night, just one night. He'd known nothing about Millie. Now he was faced with the dilemma of a child alone. *His niece*, he reminded himself.

Millie was a talker, and she talked all of the time. The more she talked the more difficult it became for him to leave her. *No. No he couldn't do that.* There was another thing he hadn't expected. He hadn't expected to be finding a man with a bullet in his head. Nor did he expect the man to be his brother. This man, the very one he'd just buried, had been killed walking across the yard, his death orphaning the girl, his niece. None of this figured into his plans. What was worse, he didn't have any plans.

For that matter, he hadn't figured on himself being shot and those damn maggots, either. Both he and his brother had been caught unawares. To Joe's way of thinking Jedediah had been minding his own affairs, walking across his yard without a care in the world other than cooking pancakes and looking after a lovely daughter. Death had come without so much as a warning. He'd woken up one morning and was shot dead by a damn coward.

The sumbitch. The sumbitch. That fellow he'd have to deal with. Sure as God made heaven and hell, he'd have to deal with him.

He thought of Brigham Larson. They'd been sitting in the shade of a magnolia, Brig watching Joseph clean the firing mechanism of a pistol. *"Sometimes things will happen without any warnin','* Mr Larson said, *"just out of the blue. When they do, and they will, remember not to hesitate. It's best you remember that the fellow that hesitates gets buried."*

Poor Jedediah, he thought as he washed the dishes. *He never even got a chance to hesitate. The sumbitch that did that to a man walking across his yard ought to be shot dead...like a sick dog.*

Joe nodded his head, agreeing with himself.

CHAPTER 6

"I prayed, you know," Millie said to him.

He turned to look at her. "Prayed, well that's...."

"Yes, I prayed for a big person. 'Cause I don't have one. That makes you an answer to a prayer. I guess you are special."

"Ah, what do I say to that? Special? I don't think so."

"You say yes. I prayed. You came."

"Ok."

"Joe. Joe," she asked, "Joe, why did somebody make my Dad dead? He didn't do nothing to nobody. I needed him."

"I don't know, Millie."

"Did somebody try to make you dead?"

"What?"

"You have a sore on your head just like my Dad."

Joe touched his still sensitive scalp. He was going to say something but couldn't think what. *Hell's fire.* He didn't know what he was going to say. Instead he just looked at her.

"Joe is somebody going to make you dead like my dad?"

"Millie, Millie....I..." He stopped talking, thought for a minute. "No," he said. "Tomorrow we're going to go look for this sumbitch. Maybe I'll ask him to stop shooting people. Maybe I'll put an end to this killing of Dads."

"What's a 'sumbitch?' Is that a man who kills Dads?"

Joe chuckled and thought the word was something that Foster Smith would use. "Yes, Millie." At the thought of Foster Smith a feeling came over him. It wasn't the first time he'd felt it. He knew this feeling instantly.

"Mind your own business, boy. You'll sure as hell live longer." *He paused then, considering.* *"Sometimes you'll have to get up and set things right. You'll have to do it simply because it's the right thing to do, your business or no."*

"How will I know when to do that?" Joe asked.

"You won't, boy. You'll just be sittin' there one day drinkin' a little black coffee enjoyin' a piece of fine apple pie and there it will be."

And there it was, bubbling up inside him like hot roof tar. He smiled to himself. It seemed a little bit odd to be the answer to Millie's prayer. But that's what she thought. Fortunately, there was more than one way to be an answer to a prayer. But he could only think of one way to answer that prayer and he thought he ought to make sure that he answered the prayer personally.

That "hot tar" feeling left him empty; some would say unnerved. Feeling unnerved was not a familiar feeling. But inside himself, in the holy of holies that governed his concept of right and wrong it kept boiling over. It was what Foster Smith had talked about. It was a need to make a something right, to balance what wasn't right with what ought to be. It pushed him.

Drying his hands, he sat down at the kitchen table, set out his firearms, and cleaned them. Millie stopped what she'd been doing and watched, noting there was an empty chamber in each cylinder.

"Joe, how come there's empty holes in your gun?"

He looked up from the oilcloth and pistol.

"Well, Millie, that's where the cartridges go," he said, as he loaded each magazine. "Sometimes you keep one open so as to not shoot yourself."

"Oh."

"Tomorrow," he continued, "we're going hunting. We're hunting a man that keeps them all filled all of the time. He knows it. For some reason I know it, too. And," he paused, "this man plays his cards off the bottom of the deck. Instead of being straight up, he takes advantage of a man's back being turned, he lays in wait, stalking him, insuring his success without endangering himself. Some days we trust, Millie, because folks earned that trust. Tomorrow isn't one of those days. Tomorrow we take care. Tomorrow we give this sumbitch exactly what he gave your Dad and me. We give him no chance at all."

Millie looked at this stranger, at whose arm she was standing. "How do we do that?" she asked.

"By taking no chances." he replied.

In the evening he checked on the sorrel. Millie went with him. He fed and watered the sorrel and the other horses in the corral. He left some oats for the sorrel to eat. Millie watched him, standing close to him. She talked the whole time about something--he wasn't sure what--and about nothing at all. He found something comforting in the chatter. Before he went inside he found his saddle and the sheepskin coat. Out of the inside pocket he pulled the blue doll with the black button eyes and red string hair. He handed it to her.

"Is that for me?" she asked.

"It is."

"How did you know I needed one of those? It's not my birthday. It's not Christmas."

"Your Dad told me."

"He did? That is so nice. He loved me lots." Her face lit up with a smile. "She's so pretty."

Joe made himself a bed on the couch then followed Millie to her bedroom to tuck her in. Near midnight he woke to find Millie sleeping at the foot of the couch on his feet. In the dark she clutched the blue doll, curled up like a puppy. Joe covered her up and went back to sleep. He dreamed of Brig Larson.

"Who ordered these, Brig?" Joseph had opened a wooden box from Colt Arms Manufacturing, prying the lid off with a screw driver. Lying in folded cloth were three SSA Colt six shooters, Army issue, walnut handles. Without thinking, he had one in each hand, balancing them, weighing them, feeling the smooth action of the hammers seating, imagining the recoil. They were beautiful. Holding a brace of pistols in his fists, he'd never been so in love in all of his life as he was at that moment.

"I did," Larson replied, looking at the almost fifteen year old boy who stood all of six feet, bony shouldered, and skinny. Larson watched as Joseph played with the action of the two pistols.

"I've taught you all that I know, boy. Those are for your birthday. Foster's idea. Foster's money, too, truth be told. When is it? Tomorrow? This will be your last day workin' for me, Joseph. You'll be on your own. Up there on the shelf is an envelope. It has twelve

hundred dollars in it. It is the last of the money that Foster and I owed your Father. Expect you ought to give it to your mother. With that our debt will be paid in full."

Brigham Larson wasn't done and he was a man who didn't often have a lot to say. "I wouldn't carry those shootin' irons in public until you have to. You're still a boy. Folks won't be expectin' it. They'll give you that. If you let them, folks'll let you finish growin' up. The time for strappin' on a six-shooter is comin' all too quick, you'll find."

"You must be joking. Oh my God!" Joseph exclaimed, and then, "Thank you, Mr. Larson. I really owe you."

"You are welcome, boy. Over under the counter is a case of cartridges. I'm throwin' it in. You ought to keep practicin', cartridges or no.

"Another thing, boy, somethin' for you to think about. I do not pretend to be tellin' you what you ought to be doin'. Sometimes it's best to let the past be in the past. Those folks that caused you grief--they're a mean bunch of bastards, not to be fooled with. Hard tellin' where you'll find them. Maybe you shouldn't even look."

"But, Mr. Larson, those folks that killed my father, they not only kept me from having a pa but my brother and sister, too. They kept my mother from having a husband. He never did anything to them. He wasn't even carrying a firearm. Packard just shot him without so much as a fare thee well. If I do not pay him a visit he'll do it again simply because he can. That's not right. That's just not right."

"Well, boy, what you are sayin' is true. But be careful and be quiet about it. Folks say that vengeance, perhaps even justice in some cases, is best served up cold. I'd add to that and say ice cold, when it's least expected, and the need for it not remembered.

"I'd remind you of another thing you ought to consider as you are makin' your way. Remember that your mother and your family need you and they don't need you dead. Fact is, dead folks aren't much good to anybody."

Joseph smiled. "Point taken," he said. "Point considered and taken and thank you. Many thanks to you. I'll always be in your debt."

"Last thing, boy. You'll find Packard on the river. Just a thought. He never worked alone. He always worked for someone."

CHAPTER 7

In the early morning, when the dew still clung to the grass like a thousand diamonds glistening in the sun, he saddled the sorrel, putting the girl high upon the shoulders of his saddle. He mounted, straddling the sorrel behind her. He rode east at first, hoping to cross someone's trail, knowing that he would probably be riding south before long. He'd judged from how the corpse had lain that the shooter had been above the house, probably on the back ridge. A six hundred yard shot, not too far; close enough to be accurate on a windless day.

Joe had to crawl inside the man's head. Questions popped up continually. *How long had he laid in wait? Had he waited? An hour, maybe? A day? A week? What about the wind? Some? A little? No wind at all? The light? Early evening would be a sure bet, especially if he shot from the shade. No sun that way. Easy shot. Just aim and squeeze the trigger.* For no reason, Joe thought of the sand sock and wished he had it with him.

It was a long shot but from where? The shooter would need an easy covered escape route, a place no one looked, a place to hide and shelter his horse. The ridge wasn't that easy to climb. A man would have to be looking for something special just to go up there. There wasn't much grass: primarily red rim rock and scrub juniper.

Joe spent all morning searching, riding back and forth along the ridge line listening to Millie's observations and studying the ground. Sometimes he walked leading the sorrel, Millie riding in the saddle. With each criss-cross he moved farther and farther back from the cliff until he found what he was looking for, just as he knew he would. Success brought a smile to his soul. An old familiar feeling washed over him and he knew he'd trailed someone like this before. He wondered who.

The shooter had lain under the low hanging limbs of a quaking asp, hidden by a stand of sagebrush, and a rock formation that rose beside it. The grass was flat where he'd set up the shot. Judging by the ground, he'd been there several days waiting for the appropriate time, the perfect conditions. *Confident bastard.* He left a casing, left it standing on its end as a marker, a reminder, a monument for those to see who knew what to look for.

Perhaps he was also an arrogant bastard. Joe thought so and kept the spent cartridge, kept it in his shirt pocket, the one with the patch sewn crosswise.

One thing bothered Joe more than he cared to admit. This shooter didn't hide his trail. Instead he was supremely confident that he wouldn't be followed, or if he was followed it wouldn't matter much. He rode a grey horse, left grey horse hair on a branch, left it on a tree trunk, left it like a signed confession. The grey had a malformed frog; the shoes were tight, though. The grey horse hair Joe kept, thinking he might need it.

The shooter did not keep to the streambeds, did not take advantage of the flat rock, didn't try to hide himself. Instead, he rode in straight lines, stopping to cook, to sleep, even to fish. He was definitely not in any hurry.

Joe and Millie, on the other hand, left the man's trail from time to time, rode back and forth across it, followed a game trail, then a creek bottom. They dry camped amid the rocks, stayed deep in the pines, moved slowly, checked and rechecked their back trail before re-establishing themselves.

Not that Joe didn't find something to worry him. He did. Studying the tracks laid out on the ground made him nervous. He had that feeling that someone was also watching him, following him. It was just too easy. So Joe continued to cut back, watched his own back trail, took three days to travel ten miles. Each day he became more anxious, more secretive. It was like a plague. He took no chances and gave none. He did not sleep much. If he slept at all, it was in fits and starts.

"Lordie Bob, boy. You're lookin' like there's a ghost or a griz behind every pine. Relax, before I club ya' over the head and put a stop to your misery and mine."

"But, sir, you said to be aware of everything."

"You are aware. Remember what you are lookin' for. Remember what you want to train yourself to recognize is somethin' out of order, out of the nature of things. Birds that bolt from their nest like God himself sent for them. Deer runnin' like the Devil was hangin' on their tail kickin' them in the rear. Muddy water in a stream that should be runnin' clear. Angry bees strikin' like a snakebit dog.

"Listen for the quiet 'cause nature ain't normally quiet. It's a bundle of noise singin' to you. Somethin's up when it's not singin'. That's when the hair ought to stand up on the back of your neck. Not now. Now everythin' is in its place hummin' along. Relax when it lets ya'. Get nervous when it tells ya' to get nervous."

All right, Foster. Joe tried to relax. Hard as he tried, in the evenings Joe would find himself moving away from the trail deep into the forest to make camp. It was slow going.

The child slowed him down. She needed breaks, needed to eat, needed to chatter. About what, he wasn't sure. He listened though. Fortunately in the evening she'd be tired and sleep wasn't long in coming.

On their third day sometime after midnight, a light streaming through the pines woke him. For a moment he lay still, not sure of what to expect, or for that matter, of what he was seeing. From where he lay he could see the sorrel on the picket line. He could see him clearly and he shouldn't have been able to, not at night, not in the middle of the night, not with his back up against a two hundred foot cliff and surrounded by lodgepole pines rising seventy five feet above the forest floor. But he could see Millie's towhead sticking out of her blankets. He could see the rise and fall of her chest. The light was that bright, so strong it cast a shadow. It was steady like a lantern, one big lantern. It was as strong a light as he remembered seeing at night in the twelve days that he could remember anything, which was not a strong endorsement. But Joe wasn't in the mood to take chances. He pinched himself to see if maybe he was dreaming. He wasn't sure these days. He could be. But it hurt. No, he was awake. He could hear his heart beating.

Slowly he pulled on his boots. They were cold on his feet. He stuck one of his extra pistols in his waistband and started crawling to where Millie lay wrapped in dreams, oblivious to the danger he felt, the uneasiness that struggled within him. At any moment he fully expected the night to erupt, to seize him and toss him away like chaff on the wind. He kept to the undergrowth, moving slowly until he reached her. It was only ten yards but it felt like a mile. It felt like forever. Carefully he gathered her sleeping form in his arms and, still keeping to the shadows, moved quietly behind the monolithic boulders that stood higher than a man on a saddle horse, big as a barn. He listened and heard the night birds, the wind in the pines, an owl on the hunt. Nothing else. The light was coming from behind the pines east of the creek. He waited, standing, a shadow within a shadow.

Millie stirred in his arms. He dared not put her down.

"What's wrong, Joe?" she mumbled.

"Somebody's coming," he whispered.

She snuggled deeper in her blanket, peering up at his face, a face hidden in the shadow of the boulder that protected them. "Really? Who? Are they dangerous?"

"Don't know."

"Well, why are we awake?"

"Can't tell."

"Well, what did you see?"

"Nothing.'"

"Nothing?"

"Just some light."

"You saw a light?"

"I did. I do."

"Where?"

"Across that creek."

Millie, all seven years of her, struggled to sit up. "Where?" she asked. "I don't see no light."

"Over there, coming through those pines. See it? Over there. It's coming from over there. You see it?"

Millie sat up in his arms, stared in the direction he was looking, then threw her head back against his shoulder and sighed.

"Joe, you're crazy. You're so crazy. That's the moon. It's just the moon. You're so crazy. You're scared of the moon."

"Moon?"

"Yeah, the moon. You got us up to look at the moon. Geez, Joe. I wanna sleep. I just wanna sleep."

Joe hesitated. "What's the moon?" he asked realizing even as he spoke it was a stupid question; he knew what the moon was.

The little girl's eyes stared up at his chin through her blankets. "You ain't never seen the moon? Mom said my dad hung the moon. Maybe he did. Said he put it right there for her to see. Don't know if it's so. Mom just said it. Sometimes she was silly. Sometimes grownups are just silly. Are they crazy sometimes like little kids? You're just teasing, aren't you? Everybody's seen the moon, not like you could miss it. It's just too big, Joe. Geez."

There it was rising above the pines, round and bright, the most beautiful thing he could remember seeing, ever. He stared at it, afraid to take his eyes off of it, afraid that it would go away in a blink. A lot of things had.

The girl in his arms had gone back to sleep, mumbling to him. She had said, "I ain't seen nobody scared of the moon. You take the cake, Joe. You sure do." And she was gone in an instant, wrapped in her dreams, wrapped warm in her blanket, secure in the arms of the most bewildered man she'd ever met. And Joe? He stared at the moon rising above the pine forest and wondered about cake and just how it was that he could take it.

Maybe, Joe said to himself, *maybe there are other things I haven't noticed because I just can't remember them.* Unfortunately, he was no less anxious, remembering that the fellow who'd shot him had been pretty quiet about it, maybe even hiding in the moonlight. Who knew? Sleep came grudgingly.

Somewhere lost in flickering eyelids, a woman came to him. It was dark, long past sundown. She was different–tall, with dark hair flowing down her back. They were on a boat of some kind, looking across a river. They listened to an owl hooting, a coyote's howl, and

across the swirling black water they watched
the rising moon, so big, so round.

"Have you ever....?" she asked him quietly.

"No, I haven't," he answered. She leaned
against him, his arms wrapped around her
waist, swaying to the throbbing of a steam
engine, listening to a paddle wheel turning,
listening to the gurgling of the thrashing,
churning water.

"Hold me," she murmured. "I don't want
this moment to pass us. I want to watch that
old moon for as long as we can."

He nodded, feeling her body leaning
against his, warm and sweet.

The thought, the dream, the pleasant feel
of it moved on and somewhere in the early
morning he lost his grasp on it. Oh, how he
wanted it back.

The sounds of Millie woke him to his
unease, to his unspoken embarrassment. The
sun was up already. He'd been tired. Now he
was no longer in a hurry, still thinking about
the long haired woman, the moon, and the
river, thinking he was hungry for something
good. He made no effort to break camp. They
just sat in the pines until late morning, eating
biscuits he made in a frying pan and fish he
helped Millie catch from the creek.

His ordeal with the moon plagued him.
Over and over he thought about it, reviewed it
in his mind. *I should have known about the*

moon, he thought, *like I know stars, like I know the sun coming up in the morning. Why didn't I?* He remembered the sweet smell of the woman's hair and suddenly knew all sorts of things about the moon and whether it hit or missed a cloud. Despite himself, he wanted to know a lot more.

Later, in the early afternoon, he picked up the trail of the grey horse. Following it, they dropped down from the flat into a canyon and finally found a road. About a mile later the road turned and led to a settlement that sat among the pines at the foot of the mountain they had just descended. *Forget about the moon*, he thought. *Tend to the business at hand.*

The sorrel, without any urging, walked up Main Street going south. On their right was a livery stable, on the north side of the barn were some corrals for holding livestock, primarily horses. Farther up the street buildings had been constructed on both sides. Millie rode quietly, leaning back against Joe, cradled between his arms, watchful.

CHAPTER 8

Sheriff William McInroe sat in the middle of his rocking chair rocking back and forth, listening to the wood creak under the oak rungs. He'd been sitting on the boardwalk in front of his office for fifteen minutes. That was his custom, a custom a man could set his pocket watch by; for having been elected by the honest folk of the Territory, he needed to be seen. So the rocker and boardwalk creaked together and he watched the people going about their afternoon business. It was two-fifteen p.m.

It was an excellent time to do so. There wasn't much trouble at two-fifteen in the afternoon, nothing that pulled him away to a desk, or took him away on horseback. The hard cases, the rowdies that plagued the west side, were waiting for darkness to crawl out of their holes. So now he could relax, enjoy the moment of peace and domestic tranquility. And relax he did, ever mindful of his rules of office. Never prowl around looking for some hard case no-account after dark; anything and everything could wait until he could see.

Never get anywhere too soon; let the bastards get away. It was better to arrive late than get shot. And last, never get yourself killed. They were simple rules really, rules to live and stay alive by. He liked them because they worked.

"Hey, Uncle." That would be his nephew, Jonesee.

"Yeah," the sheriff responded, not taking his gaze from the street.

Across Main Street an elderly man and a woman, she much grayer than he, came out of the Old Gold City Bank. They stood looking about before turning to their right and entering the two story Mirror Hotel. Next door old man Benson was sweeping the boardwalk in front of the Mercantile. It belonged to him and he was bent on keeping the boardwalk clear of dust and debris and on being outside in the sunlight.

"That's the second time that rider has passed us. Looks like he's looking for something."

"So?" Bill disliked--really hated--anyone, including his nephew, interrupting his two o'clock rock in the sun. "It ain't against any law for a man to be riding up and down the street as many times as he figures he's of a need."

"But, Uncle Bill, he's got that Johnson girl riding on the shoulders of that saddle. And Uncle, look, that ain't no ordinary saddle horse. Uncle Bill," Jonesee paused, "I got a feeling, that one I get, that one you don't never want to hear about."

Indeed, he did detest hearing about "that feeling" even more than he detested a simple interruption. If there was trouble anywhere, his sister's son seemed to know about it, sometimes before it happened. No, he didn't like it much, but he kept that boy around because he hated the thought of trouble sneaking up on him unawares even more. McInroe was convinced that his bacon had been pulled out of the proverbial fire more than once by "that feeling." McInroe took it seriously.

"You got a feeling?"

"Yeah, sorta like somebody stepping on a freshly dug grave. Seeing that rider gives me the chills." He paused. "Sorry, Uncle," he said.

The Sheriff had stopped rocking. "Don't let it bother you none, boy. Where's he going?"

"Looks like to the livery, Uncle." Jonesee paused, staring down the street. "Looks like he's putting up his horse."

McInroe let the air out of his lungs. "Well, Jonesee, you keep an eye on him. He ain't done nothing illegal yet, nothing that would land him in jail."

Six minutes later Jonesee interrupted his Uncle again. "Uncle," he said. "that fellow ain't putting up his horse. He's coming back up the street."

Bill stopped rocking for the second time. Both stared down the street at the approaching rider. But the rider didn't make it as far as the Sheriff's Office. Instead, he turned west onto Benson and disappeared behind the bank building.

This isn't good, not with Jonesee having one of his feelings, McInroe thought. Coming to his feet, "Jonesee, " he said, "hustle down to Fred's. See what that fellow wanted. Probably nothing. I'm going to see where he's disappeared to."

"I can tell you where he's goin', Uncle."

Bill looked at his nephew, waiting.

"To the Dollar," he answered. "He's goin' to the Dollar."

"Well, maybe, but we don't know for sure. You hurry. See what Fred has to say. You know where I'll be. Now hurry, Jonesee."

Sheriff Bill McInroe watched his nephew's back bobbing up and down as he ran across the boardwalk and then out into the street. *That boy might as well be talking to Fred as getting shot at the Dollar. Something just isn't right. A rider with a little girl riding in the saddle should be counted on not to start trouble. Such a man just didn't do that.*

Heaving a sigh of trepidation, McInroe stepped off the boardwalk into the street, checking his pistol as he did, shoving a round into the empty chamber. *Can't be too careful.*

Every time that kid gets that feeling somebody dies.

At the same time he didn't really care if that someone happened to be visiting the Dollar. It was a saloon. The rough edge made it their home. Nobody bothered them there, including Bill. There was no sense in it; besides the fact was some of those fellows needed killing. *Still*, he thought, *a killing is just that, a killing.* It was messy. Worse, it was in town and the folks who elected him didn't care for killings that much, especially in town.

The man Millie called Joe had ridden Main Street twice, studying every horse.

"I don't see no white horse, Joe," Millie said.

"Grey. We're looking for a grey horse."

"I don't see no grey horse neither."

"We'll try the livery. The sumbitch couldn't be far."

"Ok," she said. "What's that?"

"What's what?"

"A livery, Joe?"

He paused, thinking before he answered. "It's a hotel for horses."

"Oh, I didn't know horses had hotels."

"Well, sis, they do," he said.

The livery stable was on the north end of the town. He'd noticed it riding in. This town wasn't big; locating the stable didn't take long.

The hostler was pitching hay as they rode up. He stopped to watch them, his eyes evaluating the horse they rode. He was a skinny, jovial guy, the helpful sort, the kind that knew everybody, talked to anyone--a sort of likeable town crier. He didn't hesitate to identify himself.

"Fred's the name. Can I help you?" Everyone knew him. His 'shaking' hand was always out, his willingness to be of service, renowned.

Before Joe could reply Millie stated their business. "We're looking for a sumbitch on a white horse."

"It's a grey, Millie. Grey."

"Oh, yeah," Millie responded. "We're looking for a sumbitch on a grey horse!"

A smile appeared on the hostler's face. It was something he hadn't heard before, not from the lips of a child.

"You are, are you?" He hesitated as if wondering if it was something he could talk about, glancing up at Joe.

"There are three," he finally said, "that I know about. Two belong to a rancher two miles east of here. Nice looking pair. Well broke to a wagon. The third, he belongs to a feller that ain't from here. Not really. Folks say he's a back shooter. For hire, know what I mean? Nobody's seen it, mind you. That's just what I hear tell. A bad man. A real bad man."

Joe nodded. "Where do you reckon I could find this gent?"

"If he's in town, he'll be at the Dollar. I ain't seen him in weeks, though. Hopin' he's gone for good, I was. But when he's about, that's where you can find him mostly. The gossip is he likes to go there after he's kilt some poor soul. Sorta' to celebrate. That's what folks say. Don't know the truth of it.

"I'd stay away from him, Mister. Clean away. He's pure poison. Not a good bone in him. Know what I mean? Especially you gots a gal like this one to look after."

"Thanks," Joe said. "Where could we find this Dollar?"

"Well, sir, you ride up this here street and turn right as soon as you can. It'd be right there on Benson. Practically a stone's throw."

Joe glanced up the street, thinking about a stone's throw.

"Thanks," he said. "Thanks for the advice. We'll just have a few words with this fellow, if he's around. Then we'll stay clear."

The sorrel started with the click of Joe's tongue, moving slowly up the dirty little street. Turning right on the first street they came to, just as the hostler said, there was the Dollar. It was a nondescript building. Nothing but bare land growing a crop of cheat grass on either side. The sign was weather faded, yet across the false front was a white reminder that, indeed, here was the Dollar Saloon.

In front were two hitching rails, six horses. The last on the right was a grey.

Millie broke the silence. "Joe, there's a white horse."

"Sure looks like it, Sis."

"What should we do?"

"I reckon we should go inside and introduce ourselves."

"Ok."

Joe stepped down from the sorrel and lifted Millie out of the saddle so that she was standing next to him in the middle of Benson Street. Nothing was on his mind. Nothing of any consequence that he could comment on, should he be asked. Some folks later on talked of his irresponsibility. How a real man, someone who cared, would not take a child into harm's way. He never thought about it. It never even crossed his mind. Those mores of human decency were not part of him today, if they had ever been. The only concern he had was that there was a man inside that had shot him out of the saddle and left him for dead. Except he wasn't dead and he wasn't allowing that mistake to occur twice. *No second chances for either him or me*, Joe concluded.

And Millie? If it had been verbalized, he felt she had a right, a right of passage to see the man who'd shot her pa, who'd orphaned her, who'd stolen life experiences from her and who had left her to starve to death in the wilderness. It was, in his mind, a concept anchored in his rigid value system: black and white, right and wrong, no shades of gray. It's what Brigham Larson and Foster Smith had explained to him, all the time pressing a pistol into his hand. It was simply the way of it.

The pleasant mood of the man, Joe, was anchored in this search for equilibrium. What's more there was no doubt in him. He never even wondered if he could handle the situation, this situation, or any situation. It wasn't any different from finding a rattlesnake at his front door. He'd kill it. That's the message he received when he was ten. That's the lesson he learned when he was fifteen walking out of the general store brought up on the gospel of Foster Smith and Brigham Larson.

"You takin' more than one of those?" Millie asked, as she pointed at the pistol that hung on his right hip.

"I reckon."

"You gonna' fill the extra hole?"

"I reckon I have."

"No time to trust, huh?"

"No time this time," he answered.

In the dusty street he found comfort in small things: the unbuckling of the latches of the saddlebags, the feel and smell of leather, a pistol wrapped tightly in brown cotton, the gun oil smell of it. All so familiar, so covered in deja vu, so surreal he could almost taste it as it came welling up around his collar. Balancing the weapon in his right hand, he rolled the cylinder on his arm, stopping to make sure all chambers were loaded, flipping it around in his hand like a child's toy, enamored with the balance of it, the cold steel, the smoothness of the wooden grip. This one he placed in the holster. The displaced pistol he shoved between his belt at the small of his back, grip turned to his left hand.

The third revolver, equally treated, found a resting place neatly tucked behind his belt buckle, its grip accessible to his right hand.

"Geez, Joe," Millie said, watching his preparation somewhat in awe. "You gots more guns than a Army."

"I do, Millie. In case a war breaks out I'll be ready."

"How are you gonna shoot so many guns? You only have two hands. How many is that?"

Joe was looking down at her. "How many what?" he asked her.

"Bullets. How many bullets you gots?"

"Eighteen."

"Geez," she said.

"I know," he said. "I know what you're thinking. I hope that there ain't nineteen of those sumbitches riding that grey horse."

"You're funny," she giggled.

"Yes, ma'am. I'm funny. You ready?"

"I am, Joe."

"Well then, let's go inside and answer some prayers."

CHAPTER 9

Leaving the sorrel ground-hitched standing quietly by the grey, the two stepped up on the boardwalk that fronted the Dollar saloon. An odd couple, if there ever was one, the girl gripped the pocket of his faded pants, once black, now varying shades of grey. She was looking at the swinging doors, at the darkness within, a grim set to her jaw, then hurrying to keep up with Joe, to be safe with an unsafe man.

Parting the doors, he and Millie passed through the portal, her short legs moving quickly. Inside, Joe looked into the darkest corners, letting his eyes adjust quickly. The saloon was dark, but not so dark that a man couldn't see. And see he did. His eyes swept the rectangular room; he saw who was sitting, who was standing, and who was leaning at the bar conversing with the lone barkeeper.

Three steps inside and already he had catalogued friend and foe, measured distances, picked a place to stand. Millie, still attached to his left pocket, was the attention getter. It wasn't often a seven year old walked into a bar on the west side, a sight rarely seen by the rough riders of the American frontier. It was probably the flip of her head, the manner in which her blonde hair danced about her shoulders, the glow of her skin as she took in the scene that unfolded before her, or perhaps the child's voice, her words so foreign, so out of place, that caught their attention.

"We're lookin' for the sumbitch who rides the white horse," she announced.

"Grey, Millie. A grey horse."

"Yeah. We're looking for the sumbitch that rides the grey horse!"

They turned to the voice, everyone seeing her radiance and the dark foreboding presence of he to whom such innocence clung. Him, they understood. He carried more armament than George Armstrong Custer. There indeed was a reckoning about to unfold and there was a child directing the choir. No, she was the choir.

As quickly as they took her in and felt the shadow of death pass by, they scrambled to safety. The two men at the bar faded toward the back and out the rear door. Several stepped out the front door because it was closer. The barkeeper moved himself out of a perceived line of fire, edging farther away, also toward the front door.

Someone said casually, "Well, Ed, that'd be you." A figure stood and slowly moved away from a rear table. He held his hands deliberately away from his hips, palms up. The nearer tables were immediately vacated leaving one man wearing a grey hat sitting all alone, his back against the wall, one hand in his lap, another holding a hand of cards. Carefully he set them face down on the scarred table and stared at the girl. Those remaining in the saloon now looked at him, waiting, a room holding its breath, knowing that anything and everything could happen. They were not soon disappointed.

Joe smiled. He flipped the spent cartridge he'd been carrying in the patched shirt pocket, watched the brass casing spin, catch the light, then hit the table, rolling to the man's chest, dropping into his lap.

"Yours?" Joe asked.

There was no answer. The fellow picked it up, glanced at it, and set it on the table in front of him. It was his. He knew where it came from. He'd left it. A confidence seemed to flow from him--a confidence born of having been here before, of having been confronted before. He knew his capabilities, who he was and who he had been. Men feared him. He liked being feared, being talked about in hushed tones, and avoided when possible.

"Think that's him, Joe?" Millie asked.

"Probably."

Millie fixed her gaze on him, seeing the lone man unruffled by their intrusion.

"Are you the sumbitch that rides the wh...,
grey horse? 'Cause if you are, you killed my
dad, and we've come to kill you. We aim to kill
you dead just like you did my dad. Dead. Very,
very dead!"

Someone in the back and to the left
chuckled. It wasn't the man at the table. He
was unmoved by the girl's little speech. After
all, he knew what he could do and what he was
going to do, and laughing wasn't part of it.

Joe waited, every muscle relaxed, waiting
like a coiled snake, every fiber filled with
anticipation. He waited, a smile hanging on
the corner of his lips, knowing he'd found him,
knowing what was coming, loving it,
surrendering to it. He knew the owner of the
grey horse would have to step back or his pistol
would never clear the table. Mistake number
one. The man's second mistake was he'd either
have to stand or shoot sitting down. *Watch the
shoulder. It will be the first to move.*

And just as Joe knew he would, the rider of
the grey did stand, stepping back, coming to
his feet, making himself smaller by turning
sideways. The revolver came clear of the
tabletop. Up. Up. But to the man's surprise
and shock something struck him in the chest
just below the heart. His pistol prematurely
discharged into the tabletop. Something was
strangely wrong about this, so out of place,
disrupting the order of things. Something
slammed into his throat. Then just as quickly

something struck his forehead and the lantern of his soul went out as he crumpled to the floor.

The conflict was like a sudden lightning storm: first the flash of light illuminating the room, then thunder, then silence and the acrid pall of gunsmoke hanging in the air. Joe, the prayer answered, stood by the bar halfway down its length, a small girl clinging to his pant leg. The pistol that had come alive was seated in the holster that had given it birth. Now both hands were filled with iron; he was looking at the rest of the saloon patrons like a hawk eyeing a rat, inviting anyone to join in, begging anyone so inclined to step up.

No one accepted the unspoken invitation. No one moved in that pregnant moment of possibilities. Except Millie. She had released her grip on the pants pocket and, holding her ears against the thunderous explosions that had enveloped the room, crossed the room to the twitching, jerking, dying body and kicked him as hard as a seven year old can kick.

"You, sumbitch," she yelled and kicked him again and again, each time repeating aloud the epitaph as though it fulfilled a promise. It was a pronouncement more important than anything in the mind of a seven year old.

Laughter. The odd spectacle of the gunman and the little girl struck someone funny. The tension broke then. A man came forward, curious, inspecting the body, then pointing at the bullet holes, noting the precise pattern. He glanced nervously back at Joe who was holstering one pistol, tucking it inside his waist belt, and holding the other. Joe stood watchful, feeling, rather than seeing the girl reattach herself to his pants pocket.

"Joe, I guess we're done," Millie said to him. "Can we go? I don't like this place."

"Ok," he replied.

And just as they had entered, they left. Once out in the street Joe lifted Millie up onto the shoulders of the saddle and swung up himself. She leaned back against him.

"Joe," she said, "the pistol sort of hurts."

Without a word he removed the pistol from his waist belt, wrapped it in the brown cotton cloth, and, reaching down, hid it in the depths of the left saddle bag. The sorrel was moving. Soon Joe had both extras tucked away, fully loaded. It was no time to trust, not today. The sorrel turned the corner onto Main Street and headed north toward the edge of town.

Folks passed them on the street, walking out from the bank and the mercantile, looking at each other, wondering what was going on, looking for the cause of the latest commotion. The sheriff's nephew ran around the corner onto Benson, turning towards the Dollar looking for his Uncle. He did not notice the sorrel as it moved past him or the blonde hair fluttering up into the rider's face.

"Uncle," Jonesee yelled, reaching him out of breath. "Uncle, Fred said he was looking for that Beasley man. You know. Ed."

Sheriff McInroe nodded. "I reckon he found him."

"Geez! That's too bad!"

"Jonesee, who the hell you cheering for? The good guys or the bad?"

"What do you mean?"

"Let's go see, Jonesee. We probably won't get shot for looking. Come on."

The pair walked down the street toward the Dollar. Men were standing outside already, chattering back and forth about what they'd seen and heard. Inside they found a corpse shot four times: twice in the chest, once in the throat, and once in the head. That, in and of itself, was not noteworthy except that the shots were in a straight line. The shooter had placed the shots exactly where he had wanted them. That didn't happen very often. In fact, no one could recall it ever having happened.

"Geez!" Jonesee said to no one in particular. "He done this in less time than it took for me to run to Fred's and back. I didn't even see him leave."

"I did," said the Sheriff. "And God bless him!"

CHAPTER 10

Joe, had he known clearly who he was, who he'd been, where he was from, and what it is that he did, most likely would have prided himself on not letting himself get talked into corners, corners from which there was no escape. He would have known it was something a man watches for, guards against, even avoids like the Bubonic plague or scurvy, and, with a little experience, sees coming a long ways off. Maybe he'd also have remembered that some corners were inevitable no matter what he did, no matter how long he prepared. Maybe he'd have known that those weren't corners at all, just life, the unavoidable corners that just had to be accepted like falling rain, drifting snow, and hugs around the neck from seven year old girls.

Things were good for Joe riding up over the Red Rock Rim because he'd been there before. He readily recognized the lay of it and he especially liked the fact that he did. Mere days before he'd been following a grey horse, had a purpose, a known reason for his existence. Now that was all behind him and he was taking the girl home. Then what? That was a "what" that he hadn't considered. It was a corner he could avoid. It was for later. First he would get her home, build a fire in the cook stove, bake a little corn bread, fry up a little bacon and think about it slowly over a cup of black coffee, warm to the touch.

Millie didn't think about the future either. She did know, however, that being alone wasn't good. It wasn't fun, wasn't warm, and was full of hunger and frightening uncertainty. She'd been there before, before there was a Joe in her life. She asked Joe about it, about the "leaving" corner that to her wasn't a corner at all.

"Joe," she said, "my mom left me. I know where she is. She ain't coming back."

Joe nodded his head, listening.

"My dad, he left. I know where he is. And he ain't coming back. I know where you are, Joe," she paused. "I ain't got nobody else to be leaving me."

"Millie, I'm not leaving you," Joe said.

Those words slid out so easily, so effortlessly, with no thought at all. They were words that in the soul of the man suddenly needed saying, words that would allow a child to sleep at night and wake up to a day of sunshine, delight and smiles. They just needed saying. So without thought or regret he said them.

"You promise?"

"I promise." There it was: two words like doors shutting in a house that had many doors, gates thrown up blocking a dozen different roads to be traveled no more.

"Do you keep your word, Joe?"

"Millie," he said, "I always keep my word."

Joe missed it then; didn't hear it until later. Had he been listening, he'd have heard the key turning the locking mechanism, the tumblers falling into place.

"How can you say that?" she asked, uncertain. "You can't remember past yesterday!"

Joe smiled. "That is true, Sis. My head isn't too good at keeping a thought or remembering what my mother looked like. I don't remember what I was, not so clearly anyway, but I know who I am. I always keep my word, Millie. And you can take that to church."

"What if you forget? You could forget, you know. People forget. Some things you have forgotten."

Whoa, Joe thought. *What'll I say to that? What would my brother say? He'd know what to say. What would that be?*

He tried to remember his brother and then he did remember. He saw him sitting at his mother's table eating black eyed peas and spinach greens with his sister. He remembered. He wished he were there. The thought of Jedediah had come so naturally, so easily. He dwelled on it a little longer than usual because it felt good, because it made him so sad and so angry. Killing his killer didn't make it any better or any easier.

"Joe?" Millie said, looking up at him.

"Tell you what, Sis. Remember that little gold locket you showed to me? Remember? Believe you said it was your mother's. We get home, you get it for me. I'll fix it to my hatband. Every time I take my hat off to hang it up, I'll see it and I'll remember. If I take it off to scratch my head, I'll see it and I'll remember. And when you want it back, you'll say, 'Joe, I know you can remember. You won't forget me.' And I'll give it back to you, no worse for the wear. Fair enough?"

"Ok," she said, leaning back against him, feeling the rhythm of the horse, one step after another. She was quiet for a moment. "Do you know what, Joe?" she said. "My dad called me Sis. And he said he loved my mom and I could take that to church. Just like you, Joe. Just like you."

"Your Dad...he was a good man. A real good man, Sis. A real good man."

The next morning Millie found her mother's gold locket and, while Millie watched him, Joe attached it to the silver hatband just like he said he would. For a week or ten days, she looked for it, saw it when his hat hung on the wall peg inside the front door, or lay on the kitchen table while he fixed some bear sign or baking powder biscuits, saw it when he pulled it down on his face to shelter his eyes from the sun. Later when she no longer looked for it Joe assumed she had forgotten. But he hadn't; he remembered.

Several days later while sitting at the kitchen table he considered the gold locket himself, turning his hat, seeing the light reflect off its edges, gold and red. He sat thinking about being available and being gone, about remembering and forgetting, and about Millie walking through the front door someday, a young woman.

Irene had done that. *Irene, that's her name. Sis.* A smile came to his face. He remembered her name...and he remembered the fellow she brought home to meet their mother. Virgil. Then he thought about Millie. Some day she could bring home a Virgil, not the Virgil, but a Virgil.

He'd better teach her something: the things she'd need to know just in case he weren't there, if for some reason he didn't remember, if he couldn't remember. He'd better teach her the things that Irene didn't know, that she never learned. *How can I? Some things I don't know myself.*

"Irene, what's wrong?"
Her face was buried in his shirt, her surprisingly strong fingers were gripping his

arms, squeezing until they hurt. *She was sobbing.*

"The river's got him, Joseph. *I just know it.*" *She sobbed even more.* "Whatever are we going to do?"

He could see the "we" part, the two heads bobbing from behind the door to the back room, staring at him, staring at their mother sobbing into his shirt.

"What do you mean the river's got him?" *He wanted her to sit down, look at him, and explain.* "Irene, please, get hold of yourself. Tell me what's going on." *He forcefully held her away from himself.* *She was looking up at his face, tears running down her cheeks.*

"He's gone, Joseph. *He's been gone for five days.* *The river's got him.* *Just like Papa.* *I just know it.*"

"Just like Papa? *What do you mean?*"

"You know, Joseph. *He just didn't come home.* *He got killed playing cards: gambling, drinking, carrying on.*" *She buried her face in her hands.* *Her body shuddered uncontrollably.*

"Irene, Papa didn't get killed playing cards. He wasn't gambling. He wasn't drinking. He wasn't carrying on."

"But Momma said."

"Momma's wrong. She doesn't know."

"What do you mean?"

"Just that, Irene. Momma never knew. He wasn't drinking. He wasn't gambling. He was just standing there, his hands in front of him, minding his own business and this fellow shot him in the stomach and then in the head. He didn't even have a gun. He didn't say anything except 'There isn't anything to talk about.' That's all he said."

"How do you know this?"

"I was there."

"You were? How come you never said anything? How come you kept this all to yourself all these years?" She hit him on the arm, turning away. But she didn't walk away.

"There was no need, Sis. It wouldn't have done any good. It was best I just kept quiet. Mother had enough on her mind. And it's best you keep quiet. Those folks that killed Papa are still out there. They are alive. We don't need to be inviting trouble. We have enough. Now, what is your problem? Did you say that Virgil hasn't been home?"

"Joseph, why did you tell me this now? Don't you think I have enough to think about? Now Papa was murdered and Virgil is nowhere to be found. What am I supposed to do? I've asked everyone. He must be dead. This isn't like him...leaving without a word."

"He's been gone five days?"

"Yes. I don't know what to do."

"I'll have a look around. You relax. Pull yourself together. Take care of Morg and little Sarah. I'll be back soon as I can. You have what you need?"

"No, I don't. We need to eat, Joseph. We got nothin' in the cupboards. We got nothin'. Virgil had his wages, two months. Maybe someone robbed and killed him. That was a lot of money. Forty-five dollars."

Joseph found a twenty dollar gold piece, took it from his pants pocket and placed it in her hand, folding her fingers around it. She was startled by the gold coin.

"Joseph, I..." she said, clutching him to her. "Thank you so much, so very much." She was sobbing again, trying not to, but without success. Morg and little Sarah had come into the room, not their usual noisy little selves, their faces somber.

"Sis. Please. Get what you need. Sis, I'll see what I can do to find Virgil. He isn't dead. Do you want me to send Jedediah to give you a hand? He could help with the kids."

She shook her head no, trying to wipe the tears from her cheeks, trying to hold back the sobs.

"Ok, Sis. I want you to take care of things right here. I'll see what happened to Virgil."

Joseph reconsidered. She wouldn't. No, she couldn't. He'd better do it himself. "Right now, Sis, I'm going outside and hitch up old Juli to the buggy and we're going to town to get some fixin's. I don't want those two to know what hunger is."

He stared at her intently. "Irene, please. I don't want this to happen again. I don't want my niece and nephew to be hungry. If the need arises, get hold of me. I don't want you waiting thirty minutes, you understand?"

She nodded her head.

Finding Virgil wasn't all that difficult. He'd just been paid a week ago. With two month's salary he had money to burn, money to spend and two worthless brothers to help him. The brothers lived across the river on the east side. Joseph took the ferry.

The problem was not whether Virgil could be found, but what to do when he found him. Virgil was far too mean to just up and die, though Joseph thought Virgil's dying would make it easier for everyone. The problem was knowing where Virgil would be before Virgil knew that's where he was going. Then what? He didn't know. Have a nice brother-in-law chat? Say "Virgil, Irene is worried. Your kids are starving. Please go home." Joseph shook his head. That'd never work! Not with Virgil being a little drunk, showing off to his brothers. The real problem wasn't what to do. It was not doing it.

The bar didn't have a name, not one that could be found painted on the exterior of the building. It didn't even have paint. But everyone knew what it was, where it was, and who frequented the place. It was known by the first name of the current bartender: Hal's place, Newel's place, Grant's place. Virgil could be found there from time to time when he wasn't working at some odd job or making babies with Irene.

So could his brothers, Harold and Henry. It was home. They were raised not a mile down the road. Virgil's father and grandfather came there to have an afternoon drink and play a few hands of cards. It even had a billiards table. It had been there then. It was there now. Only the names of the bartenders had changed.

It was a box of a building, twenty feet wide and sixty feet long, set in a grove of cypress and willow trees. A few magnolia trees out front shaded the hitching rails. Joseph rode around back and looped his reins around a hitching rail. With his horse standing comfortably, he walked around the building and entered through the front door.

In the partial darkness, surrounded by smoke and low laugher and the buzz of conversation, he glanced around, then took a seat in the corner, his back against what was the front wall. A walnut bar practically as long as the building was on his left, bottles on shelves, a long mirror, behind it. There were eleven men standing, leaning against the bar. Joseph waited, listening. The bartender came. Joseph ordered a drink but did not touch it. Drinking and shooting never go together, ever. This could be a shooting. Who knows what would happen? It sure as hell wasn't going to be pleasant. He could absolutely guarantee it. Who wanted a brother-in-law calling you a slacker in public with your younger brothers listening?

He found Virgil sitting at a table more to the back than to the front. There were four others with him. Harold had gotten up to get another bottle and a new deck of cards. Virgil had one arm around a girl and the other holding a drink. They had been playing cards. Chips were scattered all over the table top. Moments later Harold returned with a new bottle and a new deck. Henry helped him sit down. Both were laughing noisily without a care in the world. This revelry went on for thirty minutes before Virgil spotted Joseph. He stopped mid-sentence, mid-laugh, and mid-gulp. Anger popped off his face like rain on the Bayou. His lips moved but he didn't say anything. He was seeing Joseph and only Joseph. His eyes were fixed upon him, his arm no longer around the girl's waist. At the first sight of Joseph he'd pushed her away. A perplexed look flashed across her face. Virgil had been caught.

Joseph flipped the leather latch off the hammer and sat staring at Virgil, getting angrier with each passing second. He forced himself to relax, to be calm, to settle himself into a cold and calculating posture. But it was difficult. Angry was what he wanted to be. He kept seeing Morg and little Sarah, their eyes big, their stomachs empty, their mother crying, thinking their father, her husband, was dead. It's hard being twenty-six and not liking another man's choices. Brigham Larson had said a man is entitled to have choices, to do as he pleases...except when he makes it hard for other folks. "Then," he said, "maybe not." This was a "maybe not."

"What the hell are you doing here?" Virgil was staring right at him, his voice loud. In an instant his embarrassed anger had boiled over the top. Joe could see it, hear it. He thought, Now comes the big talk, the part where Virgil convinces himself that he's every bit the man he wants to be and isn't.

Harold and Henry turned to see who Virgil was speaking to.

"I'm trying to talk myself out of killing you," Joseph said. What else could he say? Everyone heard. Men ran, suddenly fleeing. The bar was clear; the bartender gone. No one was sitting at the tables in between them. A chair had been tipped over. Chips were scattered and face cards littered the floor.

Virgil came to his feet, a little drunk, a lot unsteady. At the same time he was trying to pull a big dragoon pistol out of his waist band, a gun far too big, too heavy, too long, and too unwieldy for his hand strength. His first shot was rushed; the slug tore into the table top. The discharge made an awful sound. Harold and Henry had a surprised look; they made every effort to get out of the way, drunk or no. Harold fell over his chair, and rolled onto the dirty floor.

Joseph's reaction was to shoot the dragoon. It was certainly big enough. His first shot hit it where the cylinder and barrel met. The second struck only the cylinder. The pistol went flying, leaving a broken thumb and two dislocated fingers. It looked ugly. It surely must have hurt.

In the bedlam that followed the hammers of two Colt SAA were pulled back, locked, the metallic sound followed by a deathly silence. The acrid smell of gun smoke hung in the silence along with the smell of burnt tobacco, and the reek of corn liquor.

"You finished, Virgil?" Joseph looked right at him. Two muzzles that must have looked like the mouths of bear caves were pointed at his belly. "Tell your brothers to throw them or your pa will be burying two sons tomorrow morning."

Virgil stammered, "Please, Joe?" Anger had turned to begging.

"Harold and Henry, you in or out?" Joseph said, his voice surprisingly calm.

The brothers came to their feet slowly, each seemed to be wondering what the other was thinking, what the other was going to do. Virgil decided it for them.

He said, "Throw the pistols, boys." Virgil held his thumb and fingers in his one good hand and stared straight at Joseph, waiting for the hammers to drop. In the silence his brothers did as instructed, though they didn't appear to like it much.

Joseph was slow to speak but when he did the room listened. "Virgil, this is the way it is. You have a woman at home who thinks you are dead. You have two youngin's that haven't eaten in who knows how long. And you are here in a Cajun bar throwing money at your brothers like you had it to burn." Joseph paused, looking at him like he was a cockroach. "You can be a husband. You can be a father. Or you can be here. If you are here, I'm here for you. Do you understand? This is your warning. You will not break my sister's heart." Joseph continued, "There will be no second chances, Virgil. There is no tomorrow. There is now. So choose. Pick up the gun or get yourself home."

Blood was seeping from the fingers of Virgil's hand.

"I said choose, Virgil."

"All right. I'm leaving."

"No. The choice is to be a husband. To be a father. Or die. Which is it?"

"What?"

"You heard me. Choose."

No one likes to be forced to choose. No one. Especially in a public bar with his brothers looking on. But the pistols were not wavering. They were pointed right at his belly.

"All right."

"All right, what?"

"I'll be a husband. I'll be a father."

"Then get out of here. Your brothers and I are going to have a conversation. And if, when I step out of this bar, you are still here the deal is off. Get moving."

Virgil circled the table and the chair knocked onto its side and walked out the front door, glancing back at the mess he was leaving behind.

Joseph looked at Virgil's brothers. "One of you is Harold," he said. "The other, Henry. Both of you heard Virgil's choice. If he does not keep his word I will settle up with him...then I am coming for you. Unless, of course, you want to settle up right now. If so, be my guest. Pick up your pistols and let's go to dancing."

"Right," Harold said with not a little sarcasm. "You have two pistols pointed at us and you give us a choice? What chance is that?"

Instantly, Joseph shoved one pistol in his waist band, the other in the holster. "Pick 'em up," he said. "Send for the fiddler. Open the ball. I'm ready to dance."

"You..."

"Harold," Henry interrupted. "Keep your head. Don't be stupid. Let's get ourselves out of here. There's nothing to be gained by dying.

It's a trap. We ain't in his league. We ain't never gonna be. Move. Let's get out of here."

Harold walked in front of Henry, with Henry pushing. They walked straight for the door and neither looked back. Neither picked up his firearm. Harold and Henry walked out the front door. Virgil was nowhere to be found.

In the gloom Joseph slumped down in his chair. He looked at the amber colored drink still in the glass, unspilled. No, he said to himself. Not now. This might not be over.

CHAPTER 11

Joe's decision, his newfound preoccupation with teaching, educating, and preparing a seven year old who hardly wanted to sit down for sixty seconds or sit still for something less than that, was not greeted with wild acceptance.

"Why do I need to count?" Millie asked. "It's hard. It's really, really hard. I don't like it much."

"So you'll know how many cows you got."

"Cows?"

"Say you bought yourself ten cows and a fellow comes up and gives you two, telling you it's ten. You won't know two ain't ten and you'll lose eight cows. He'll steal you blind, girl, if you can't count."

Oh," she said, and she learned to count cows.

"Why do I need to read?" she asked. "It's hard. It's really, really hard. I don't like it much."

"Well," he said, "say a fellow comes up to you and says he wants to buy two pigs and a saddle horse. You say, Ok. I'll sell you two pigs and a saddle horse. So he draws up a writing saying he's buying and you're selling him ten cows. You sign it. Make your little X right at the bottom. He takes two pigs and a saddle horse because that's what you think you sold him. Later he comes back on the saddle horse and takes ten cows because that's what the writing says you sold him. You didn't know it 'cause you can't read."

"Ok," she said. She started to learn to read, starting with little words like "cow" and "pig" and "cat" and "dog. She learned the alphabet from A to Z and what those letters sounded and looked like.

"Why do I need to learn to cook?" she asked. "It's hard. It's really, really hard. I don't like it much."

"Well," he said, "if you can't grill up a pancake and fry some bacon, you can't eat and you'll die. If you're dead you can't count cows and people will steal from you. Nothing you can do about it. Do you understand?"

"No," she said.

"Ok. If you don't eat you'll die. If you're dead, people will steal your cows. Understand?"

"No. Why would they do that? It's mean."

"Sis, if you don't cook, you can't eat and if you can't eat, you can't smile in the morning. So cooking is all about smiling. Got that?"

"I think so. I'm not sure."

"Let's start there, girl."

And so they did. She learned about a pinch of salt, where wild onions grow, how to pick raspberries so as not to get stabbed to death. They cooked biscuits and ate them warm out of the oven, dipped in hot butter. He watched to see if she was smiling more. She was.

School was never out. And Joe was busy. If he was not listening to numbers, he was listening to the recitation of words. And that was only the first week. There was more, as there always is.

"Joe?" There was unmistakable alarm in Millie's voice. "Joe?" The voice was more shrill.

Joe stepped inside the kitchen door, a white porcelain dishpan in his left hand. He looked at her, a small waif of a girl, tears beginning to form at the edges of her eyes.

"What's wrong, Sis? What's the matter?"

Millie saw him, ran across the room grabbing him about the waist, clutching him to her. Unsure, he knelt beside her.

"What's wrong, Sis? Why are you crying?"

"I couldn't see you, Joe. I couldn't see you. I woke up and I couldn't see you."

"Well, Sis, here I am." He stood, patting her head. "I was thinking you'd be awake soon and that we'd have to feed that coyote in your tummy, the one that's always singing for more to eat, more milk to drink. That one. The more, more, more one."

"I am hungry, Joe."

"I thought you might be. And I thought that after some grits and eggs we'd go see how that sawed off runt of a pony of yours keeps getting out of the corral. I know he's not jumping the fence so we'll have to see how he's doing that. Maybe he's magic. Maybe he's growing wings. What do you think?"

She hesitated. "I don't think so."

"Me, neither. Do you want to interrupt your busy morning and come with me?"

"I do," she said nodding.

"Are you going to bring Black Eyed Bessie with you?"

"I am."

"Good. Go wash up. Run a brush through that hair of yours. Find your hat and I'll see to the grits, eggs, and cakes. Or are you thinking you'd rather work yourself around some baking powder biscuits?"

"Biscuits, Joe."

"Biscuits it is, Sis. Now be about your chores."

She was off like a fourth of July rocket to find her hat and Black Eyed Bessie, and to wash her hands and face. Brushing her hair was another problem; she couldn't find the brush. So Joe found it and helped her brush the rats out of her hair.

Millie helped dry the dishes, standing on a stool beside him, telling him about a skunk that had lived in the barn and a badger that had gotten into the chicken coop and helped himself to eggs, legs and pulley bones. To Joe's surprise they didn't lose one cup, not one dish, though she did get a little wet. How she did that was a puzzle.

Afterwards they explored the corral for holes, finding none. Finally they decided that the "damn" horse knew how to open the gate. That mystery solved they went in search of berry bushes, chokecherry trees, wild onions, and the turnips her father had planted.

"Stop Millie! Stop! Don't move. Hold still. Hold very still."

Millie turned to look at him. Joe swooped her up from the ground like she was a sack of flour about to get wet. He did a hasty retreat of several steps before he set her down.

"What's wrong, Joe?" she asked, looking up at him.

"You almost stepped on a snake, Sis. Look." He picked up a rock and tossed it at a rotting log. Immediately a buzzing, rattling noise erupted. "See it? It's a big old prairie rattler. Snakes are something you have to look out for all the time."

"I don't want to look for snakes, Joe."

"Me, neither, Sis. But they are out here. Most anywhere. And they can hurt you. So we need to know where they are. We need to be looking for them. Understand?"

"No," she said hesitating, "snakes scare me."

"And they should. Look at it this way, Sis. We find a rattlesnake in the house, in the garden, even in the barn, we kill it. It's our house. It's where we live. Out here we're in their house. This is where they live. So we need to know where they live and what to do when we find them so we can avoid them."

He glanced at her, thinking he was probably giving her too much information. "Sis," he said, "do this. If you hear a rattler talking, shaking his buttons like crazy, stop. Stop right away. He's saying, 'Millie, don't step on me.' Find where he is with your eyes and back slowly away. Come and get me and I'll deal with him. All right?"

"Ok. Because this is their house?"

"Because this is their house. Whenever you can, just leave them be. Do not play with them. Do not tease them. Have nothing to do with them. Just leave them be."

"Ok, Joe. Did my mom do something wrong? Is that why a snake bit her?"

"I doubt it. What was she doing?"

"Picking berries. Just like you and me."

"Sometimes, Sis, a snake can be going along minding its own business, not knowing someone is about to step on them. Maybe your mom never saw the snake that bit her. Maybe the snake didn't see your mom until he was stepped on. He probably bit her out of surprise. Being stepped on probably hurt him. It sounds like an accident to me. When it comes to snakes we want to avoid accidents if we can."

Millie nodded, swinging Black Eyed Bessie back and forth, watching the snake. "Are we going to kill this one, Joe?

"I am." And he promptly shot the snake through the head.

Millie watched its thrashing body.

"We killed it in its house, Joe."

"We did, Sis. I don't mind you stepping on a dead snake. It's the live rattlers that I worry about. This one you don't have to worry about any more. Remember this, though, if there is one there could be more."

"Ok, Joe. Then we should go?"

"We should be about our business. No use inviting trouble."

"What is our business, Joe?

"Cows, Sis. You're a cowgirl. We raise cows. We sell them; then we buy you a dress, a saddle, and some more cows. That's the cow business."

"Can we buy some shoes too, Joe?"

"Yes, Sis. We'll buy you a pair of shoes."

That was Monday.

Tuesday, in the afternoon, he saddled her sawed off, short legged, black pony and the sorrel and they explored the meadows below the house and barn. Toward the end of the meadow the road turned east. They kept moving south, climbing a ridge onto a plain of grass then dropping down into another meadow, looking for water. They found a water hole but no livestock, just crows and blackbirds.

"There's something wrong here, Sis."

"What? I don't' see nothin."

"I don't know."

Joseph and Millie sat their horses on the rise overlooking trees that surrounded a seep spring. At one time it had been well used. The small spring fed a small creek that wandered off a few hundred yards and died away, disappearing into the red earth. There was plenty of grass all around but no cows, no sign of deer, no antelope.

"Millie, you see any cows?"

She looked about. "No," she said.

"Back over the ridge, how many did we see?

"Thirty-six."

"But none here?"

"None."

"Why do you think?"

"Geez, Joe. I don't know."

"Let's have a look." They circled the spring, giving it a wide berth, seeing nothing out of order except that there was no livestock of any kind nearby.

"Joe, why don't we just ride over there and look? Why are we riding around it? How are we going to know what's in those trees unless we ride over there?"

"Well, Sis, do you like going into a dark room after midnight not knowing what's in there first?"

Millie shook her head slowly. "No, I don't," she said.

"Me, neither."

Joe sat for a moment watching the trees. "Millie," he finally said, "do you see those two black spots in that cottonwood? Over there on your left. Do you see that?"

"Yes."

"Here," he said, handing her her father's binoculars. "Have a look through these. Tell me what you see."

She took the glasses, looked through them, focused them as she'd been taught. "Joe, it looks like two little, black dogs in a tree."

"Did you ever see a dog climb a tree?"

She looked at him, laughing. "No, Joe," she said, "I haven't."

"Me, neither. What do you think we're looking at then?"

"Two bears. Two black bears. They are so cute. Can we go down there and help them out of the tree?"

"No. I don't think so."

"Oh, why not? They are stuck up a tree."

"Because their mother put them there. Probably saw us. Put them there to get them out of danger. Now she's watching us to see what we are going to do. She's been chasing all of the livestock away. She means to chase us away, too."

Millie was looking at him disappointedly.

"Sis," he said, "never get between a mother bear and her cubs. Ever. She'd sure enough try to kill you just to get to them. She thinks you'd be a danger to her babies."

"Well, what are we going to do?"

"We'll ride over here every day for three or four days. We'll fire off a couple of rounds and make a lot of racket. She'll probably put her babies up a tree each time. She'll start worrying, then she'll move her babies somewhere safe because she'll see us as a danger. Mothers are like that."

"Are fathers like that, Joe?"

"They are."

"Are you like that, Joe?"

"I am, Sis."

That was Tuesday. Wednesday was spent fixing hinges on barn doors, the stairs to the hayloft, and attaching a hook for a gate that a horse couldn't open without some human assistance.

CHAPTER 12

Rebecca Marchant was concerned. She was always concerned. If it was not about Mrs. Jensen's rheumatism and who would visit her, it was about the church bazaar and who would bake the pies and play the fiddle. Perhaps it was this concern that made her a good woman. And she was good, as good women go. It can be argued with some validity that it was upon the shoulders of "good women" like Rebecca Marchant that communities built grammar schools, fire stations, libraries, and elected sheriffs to keep the peace and to protect the "decent folks" from the "indecent" ones.

It was this concern on the part of Mrs. Marchant that brought her across the street and up onto the boardwalk to speak with Sheriff McInroe. It was two-eighteen p.m. He'd been rocking for three and one half minutes, having gotten a late start. Sheriff McInroe had his own concerns, or certainly the town's concerns, on his mind. It seemed that someone had been stealing Dee Willams' cabbage. Cabbage stealing was what occupied

Sheriff McInroe's thoughts when Mrs. Marchant interrupted his thinking.

"Sheriff McInroe, I need to speak with you," Rebecca called out as she approached.

I'll bet you do, the sheriff thought as he looked up to see who'd called his name. "Oh, afternoon, Mrs. Marchant. What concerns you this afternoon?" he said, ever mindful of the public that elected and paid him. "Or, should I say what concerns you concerns me, and what might that be?"

He turned. "Jonesee, get...." He looked for the boy, who, for the first time today, was conspicuously absent. *Damn that boy*, he thought, wondering about the timeliness of his sudden disappearance. He turned his attention to Mrs. Marchant.

"Pull that chair over here by me, Ma'am, and tell me what's on your mind."

"Out here?"

"Sure. It's where I am."

"But shouldn't we speak inside? In your office? This is business, Sheriff. I've come to speak with you in your official capacity."

"No. No, Mrs. Marchant. It's the two o'clock hour of the day. At two I need to sit out here and let folks know I'm on the job."

She glanced at him to see if she'd heard him correctly and concluded that she had. He looked to be dead serious.

"Now, pull up that chair and we'll talk. You'll tell me what's on your mind."

"Are you sure?" she questioned, feeling too public, so out in the open and vulnerable to people's glances. She was not at all sure she liked the feeling.

"Yes, ma'am, I am. Now pull up that chair."

Reluctantly Rebecca did so.

"Now," seeing that she was settled, "what's on your mind?" he asked.

"It's the Johnson girl."

"The Johnson girl?"

"Yes, Jedediah and Abby's child."

"They're both dead," the Sheriff said.

"Yes, they are. Everybody knows that."

"What's the problem then?"

"She's with that man."

"So? It seems like they know each other. Is there a problem?"

"He's a.... he's a brigand."

"A what?"

"A brigand."

"What's that?"

"A brigand? Well, Sheriff, it's an outlaw. A man without morals. A criminal. He killed someone with a gun. In this very town. He's a killer, Sheriff. He marched right into the Dollar with that child standing beside him and shot a man in cold blood. Good Lord, Sheriff, you know this."

""In cold blood, Rebecca? He shot Ed Beasley. He did you and every citizen of the Territory a favor. Hardly in cold blood.

Beasley was a cold blooded, cold hearted, shoot folks in the back, bastard. Excuse the language. We'd have hung him except nobody could prove it. This fellow, whoever he is, had the proof and the inclination to put an end to Beasley. He shot the very man that killed Jed Johnson. I'd say he was a saint."

"Sheriff, you are impossible. You are! He took Millie into a bar, a den of iniquity. It is a house of spirits. Men drink, play cards, curse. It's the worst in the Territory. And there in her presence he shot and killed this man. And, Sheriff, he stood there while that child kicked and swore at the deceased. That's what I heard. You ask Fred. He'll tell you."

"And that's what you're concerned about?"

"Yes."

McInroe chuckled. "She did call him a son of a bitch. And that is what he was. No doubt."

"Sheriff!"

"That's what I heard, Rebecca. That what you heard?"

"Yes."

"Well, Rebecca, what do you want me to do about it.?"

"Arrest him. Turn the child over to me. I can properly care for her. She needs proper care."

"Arrest him? For what? Killing a killer? Rebecca, this ain't happening. And if it is happening, it ain't gonna be me that does it.

Do you realize what you are asking? They say he jerked and fired four times after–hear me? I say, after Beasley had his pistol out, the hammer pulled back with his finger on the trigger. Good grief, Rebecca, I can't even get up to the table that fast. Know what I'm saying?"

"But, Sheriff, he isn't her father. She's just a child."

"Rebecca, you ain't her mother, neither. And you don't know who he is or who he ain't. They look a lot the same. Same light colored hair, same shape of face. Same eyes. I sure as hell don't know who he is, but I'll tell you this. I saw them coming into town that day. That Johnson kid sitting up there on the shoulders of that saddle looked as much at home as any kid I've ever seen. I'll go you one further; I didn't see it but that kid standing by that feller in a gunfight is safer than she'd be if she were sitting in this chair come Sunday Resurrection Morning. Rebecca, I don't know nothing but if I didn't know any better, I'd think that girl has pretty much tied herself to that man."

"Sheriff, please. How..."

"No, Rebecca. No. I surely admired your husband before the pox took him. I did. We miss him and his thoughts. I admire you taking care of those two boys of yours, you being alone. I know you were best of friends with Abby Johnson before she was snakebit. I know you care about that kid of hers. Really care. But, Rebecca, I think you're gonna' have to talk Millie Johnson out of that man. I don't think you can do it. Not because of that fellow, either. I don't think you can convince Millie she shouldn't grow up with him around keeping the wolves away from her porch. I do not."

"We'll see."

"I expect we will."

"I'll talk to him, reason with him."

"I believe it."

"This isn't over yet, Sheriff." Rebecca stood up.

"I believe that, too," the sheriff replied.

"I think you are wrong."

"I may be."

"Then Bill, why don't you do something?"

"Rebecca, that man has done nothing wrong."

Speechless, Rebecca turned and huffed off. Sheriff McInroe smiled to himself, rocking in the afternoon sun. This was sheriffing at its best.

"How long will you be gone?" Mary Rodgers asked.

"I don't know," Rebecca said to her. "It takes a big day to get there, so a big day back. A day there. So, three days. A short trip. If something happens, longer."

Rebecca was packing, getting everything ready. So far she had provisions enough for a week: oats for the horses, beans, some jerked meat, a loaf of bread, clothing for the heat, for the cold, for just in case. She never knew how much to pack but it was far better to have too much than too little. Mary Rodgers sat in Rebecca's kitchen sipping cool water from a glass and watching her.

"What could happen--that's what worries me," Mary said.

"I don't know. Who does? A horse throws a shoe, comes up lame, breaks a leg. The wagon could lose a wheel. Hey, it could rain or snow, God forbid, it's August. So I think short. I plan long." Rebecca stopped what she was doing and looked at Mary. "I sure appreciate you keeping my Jesse, Mary. I do. You're a saint. Really. Just the best."

"I wish you'd take him with you. Not that I mind having him. I don't. You need someone to go with you. That's a long ways. And you said it. Anything can happen and it usually does. I remember Abby and Jed coming back once to get a cross cut saw because a tree had fallen across the road. There was no way around it. Remember? She was pregnant."

"Thanks, Mary, for the thought. But Jesse's so young. Too young. Nine is just too young to be traipsing around in tall timber. If I come to a downed tree I'll just turn around. I do remember that now. I'd forgotten. Abby stayed with me a week while Jed cleared the road."

"Jesse's not that young, 'Becca. Think. A woman alone? It's simply not safe. It's crazy is what I think. Not too very smart. It's just asking for trouble. So you better go expecting it."

"I'll be all right, Mary. Goodness. It's only thirty miles. I've been to Abby's place. More than once. When Millie was born, remember? And before that, too."

"Yes, but you're talking forever and a day. That was a long time ago. That girl is six, seven years old. That's a long time, 'Becca. Today is today. Who knows where the big bad wolf is hiding? Or what he looks like. Besides do you know what my Fred told me? Somebody is fixing to get a court order getting that child out of harm's way. He heard that that Terrell fellow was going to old Judge Dixon, she being an orphan and all. If you just wait maybe it will all be taken care of. Who knows, right?

"All the more reason for me to go get her. I certainly don't want to see the Court take her. What business is it of Terrell's, anyway?"

"You know what I heard? Fred says that Terrell may be the one that had Millie's dad killed. It's just talk but there could be some truth to it. It wouldn't surprise me none."

"Oh, God in Heaven!" Rebecca exclaimed. "Mary, if Terrell goes out there, there could be a lot of shooting, a lot of trouble." Rebecca stood staring at Mary, her hand over her mouth. Both women were silent. Rebecca broke the silence.

"Mary, please stop fretting. Really. If I'm not back in a week come and get me. Most likely I'll be there tomorrow night, spend the next day packing Millie's things, and be back here the next day. Three days tops." Rebecca paused. "When is that Terrell going to see Judge Dixon?" she asked.

"Fred said he thought he'd already got the order. Whoever he talked to said to expect a shooting war like yesterday. 'Becca, nobody knows that fellow that took Millie into the Dollar. No one has seen him before. No one has ever heard of him. He could be anybody. Nobody knows what he'll do if Terrell pushes him even a little. Nobody expects he'll just turn that girl over to Terrell, not after what he did to Ed Beasley."

Mary Rodgers stopped talking for a moment, fixing her long tresses, pushing at the pins in her hair. "Becca, you ought to hear all the talk about that man. Every day Fred comes home with another tale. Someone thinks he could be that kid from the crossing at Chain Canyon. The one that killed all those men and then vanished. No one knew who that was, either. Somebody said he could be a man he heard of in New Orleans that blew up a big river boat with everyone on it and disappeared into the night. No one knew who did that either because no one survived to tell.

"There is a story he came from California where he held up stage coaches, stole payroll money from the gold mines. No one knew or found that man, either. They said he just disappeared. Someone else said he came from South Africa. Can you believe that? Said that man held up banks, stole silver and diamonds and such, then left the country. Nobody knows, not really. He was never caught. You'd just never believe the stories. 'Course Fred remembers them all and passes them on, bless his heart. He's just about the first to know."

Rebecca was looking at Mary, thinking. "I'd really better hurry. Seems I'm already going too late as it is." Mary stood up and hugged her.

"Be careful, Rebecca," she whispered. "Be really, really careful."

CHAPTER 13

Rebecca Marchant started for the Johnson Valley ranch early Wednesday morning, her thoughts a jumble. The evening before she'd taken Josh to the Pearls' home and Jesse to the Rodgers'. Neither of her friends thought she was doing right. In fact, they both thought she was out of her mind. "Too dangerous," they said. Mary hadn't said any more to her, except to tell her that Fred had told her that Judge Dixon had signed the order and Mr. Terrell had it. She didn't know what it said. No one did. No one had seen it.

Last night after Mary had gone home to fix Fred his supper it had been so peaceful, like the calm before the storm. She had taken Josh to Sally Pearl's house and sat on her porch talking with Sally. Rebecca loved that porch. It was long like her mother's, extending around both sides of the house. Her mother's porch had been white, made from Maine's finest oak and white washed every spring. Sally's was made of pine. Still, it was beautiful to sit out on an evening, a slight breeze smelling of pine drifting off the mountain and keeping the mosquitoes down. Sally had given Rebecca her opinion. Clearly.

"Mind your own business." Sally had said. "'Becca, who are you to be solving everyone's problems? You ought to just leave well enough alone. Life is just what it is, harsh, tough. Who do you think you are 'Becca? Just who do you think you are?"

Who did she think she was? Millie wasn't her daughter. Simple as that. But she was Abby's. Maybe, she thought, in all of this mess she could lend a hand, help Abby by helping her daughter. Abby was there for her boys. She was there when she broke her arm falling off a horse, when Sam was so sick, when he died of the pox. There was that.

"Rebecca," she said. "Maybe the child doesn't need saving. Did you ever think of that? You don't know. You are assuming a whole lot. What about that man? What about him? Have you thought about him?"

"I'll reason with him," Rebecca said. "What man living can take care of a seven year old girl? One that 's not even his. I'm sure he'll see the way of it."

That's what she'd said. But Sally wouldn't leave it be. She had looked at her in that way Sally could look when she thought you were crazy.

"Not this one 'Becca. This one you don't know. Not all men are the same. Some have rocks in the belfry."

"That's bats, Sal."

"Same thing: bats, rocks, chipmunks. I heard this one is all sorts of trouble. They say he smiled at that Beasley before he shot him dead. Smiled! What does that tell you? He hardly said nothing to anyone, that girl hanging on his pocket like she was attached. Nobody has ever seen him before. Not in these parts. Rebecca, this is trouble ringing a bell and you aren't listening."

"All the more reason to get that child, don't you think?" Rebecca said.

Sally didn't say anything to her for a moment. The silence stood between them. "Your mind is made up," Sally finally said. "I'm just flapping my lips getting my exercise breathing."

Rebecca knew Sally was right. But so was she. She couldn't ignore the man. The one with not one lick of common sense. He'd taken the child right into the Dollar, right into the middle of a gun battle. He had placed a seven year old in harm's way, inches from death, and who knows what else. *Such an idiot.* Rebecca had no choice. It was Abby's daughter. *Pretty, bright Abby.* And now Terrell was taking a hand in it with all those men and guns and horses. He might have gotten the Order but the Order wasn't about Millie. Who'd be looking out for a mere child? It had to be her. There was no one else. *I must stop thinking. I'll drive myself crazy.*

In the early morning darkness the timbered mountain rose up before her like a black foreboding wall. Soon she was in the tall pines, thick and dense, that stretched themselves hundreds of feet above her. Thirty miles to go. The horses followed the road, in and out and around, mile after mile, hour after hour. At noon she stopped, watered the horses, grained them, and let them rest. It was just an hour, then she continued on, lost from sight in the forest primeval, hidden in shade and shadow.

The team, blinders on, plodded forward only able to see what was in front of them. Rebecca sat on the board above the jockey box, her fingers barely gripping the ribbons. Sometimes she dozed. Other times she thought, letting those thoughts run, interrupted when a wheel hit a rut, a rock, a pothole, each time jerking her back to the present.

Rebecca quietly cursed herself. Abby had passed and she hadn't even known about it. It was weeks afterwards that Jed Johnson had come down out of the hills, a shadow of a man, a small waif of a five year old with him. Millie would not talk to anyone. Jed had purchased some supplies and some rock candy for Millie. He'd informed the sheriff and he'd stopped by her cabin as he was leaving town.

"What happened?" she asked, refusing to believe what she was hearing.

"I don't know," Jed replied. "Not really. I wasn't there. I wasn't with her. I should have been, Rebecca. It all happened so quickly. We were in the barn, Millie and I, oiling harnesses, repairing the traces, re-lacing a collar. I heard her scream. Something she doesn't do. She'd been picking berries. I don't remember what—gooseberries maybe, currants, chokecherries. She was on the other side of the house. Up toward the red ridge by the seep spring. You know where I mean."

Rebecca did know. She'd been there with Abby a year before. It was so unreal to hear Jed describe this event to her.

"I ran, leaving Millie standing in the barn with a can of oil. I ran as hard as I could. I found her sitting by an old currant bush, holding her neck with her hands. She was pale, shaking. In the bush was an old timber rattler. Big as I have ever seen. I blew his head off.

"Abby was grabbing for me with her hand. 'Jed, Jed,' she said. 'He got me. He got me bad.' She was staring up at me like I was supposed to do something. I didn't know what to do. A little blood was leaking between her fingers from her neck. She said to me that she didn't have much time. I asked her to let me see. She said, 'no.' She just wanted me to listen to her. I tried. She knew she was dying.

She could feel the poison, she said. She asked me where Millie was. I told her the barn. That's what I said, 'the barn,'" he paused, remembering more.

"Abby said for me to take care of Millie. I said I would. She said how much she loved me. She said that over and over again. I told her I loved her too. She asked me to hold her so I did. She told me she was cold. She said you were a good woman, Rebecca, that if I needed help with Millie, you'd be there for me." He looked at her then.

"She asked again about Millie, told me that Millie would be afraid and that I needed to help her not be afraid. I don't know what I said about that. I can't remember. Nothing, I guess. She told me she was sorry to be leaving me like that. I told her it was ok and that I wasn't going to let her leave. She said she was cold, so very, very cold.

'Then she was shaking. She passed out. I picked her up and carried her to the house but she was gone. When I got her there she wasn't breathing. All I could hear was Millie crying all alone in the barn. It was like I couldn't do anything. But I got Millie; I brought her into the house. There was nothing I could do."

Jed Johnson wept then. Unable to deal with his loss, he turned and left her standing on her poor excuse for a porch-- he, bereft of a wife, Rebecca bereft of a friend, neither able to bear the pain.

Suddenly the wagon jolted hard, nearly turned over, then righted itself. The team plodded on following the dim road, the same road used by Jed Johnson and Millie. At first when Jed and Millie came to town, he didn't come by or, if he did, he didn't stay long. Later he brought Millie to play with Josh while he purchased supplies from Benson Mercantile and posted a letter or two. Maybe he had a drink at the Dollar but she didn't think so. She'd never seen him drink.

A year later he began stopping by regularly. He had come by every month but the winter months. He must have thought that a year was long enough to mourn. She'd begun to look forward to those visits. Now Abby had been dead two years--no, over two years. Rebecca started crying, tears leaking from her eyes and running down her face.

Abby had been with her when Jesse was born and Josh, too. She was the midwife for her boys, just as Rebecca had been for Millie. That had been fun, laying the baby girl on her mother's stomach, cleaning her, bathing her. Abby was so happy.

It hadn't been fun when Sam got sick. Abby had been there for her, night after night, day after day. At first Rebecca had worried that Abby would get the pox but Abby said never, and never it was. They were such dark days before he died, when he died, after he died. Josh had been two and never knew his father. Jesse was four. He said he didn't remember much. Maybe he didn't want to remember. Sometimes she was angry at Sam for leaving her alone to raise two boys. It wasn't like he chose to die. But still, it would have been easier if he hadn't.

After Jed started stopping by her cabin once a month, she didn't think of Sam as often, except maybe when she looked at Josh a certain way and saw his dad in him. Jed brought tales of ranch life, of Millie's horse, of branding, selling the steers, and buying bulls, of looking for a dog and maybe a house cat to keep the rats company. There were stories of the badger who'd gotten into the hen house and got all but six chickens, the skunk who had taken up residence in the corner of the barn, and the baby magpies that Millie was feeding worms and grasshoppers.

Two months ago he'd suggested that they marry, that they combine their various assets and talents in the name of a better life "for all concerned." She'd expected he might. They had talked around it. But she didn't know. Sam was still in her heart as much as Abby was in Jed's--Jed's feelings were all about Abby as they should be. He'd suggested that they carve out a small space in their hearts for each other. That was almost three months ago. Later she'd found out from Jed about Becker's offer to sell and that Terrell wanted to buy both Becker's place and Jed's. That was four weeks ago at her kitchen table. She started to cry again. Four weeks ago she'd said yes. She'd have been married now. Four weeks ago she'd learned a lot over cornbread and bacon.

"Terrell wants to buy you out?" she'd asked. *"Really?"*

"So he says."

"What are you going to do? Does he know about the Becker Place?"

"No. I didn't tell him. If he knows, he found out from someone else. But he was after Becker, too. Not just the Valley. That man wants everything."

"What did Becker sell you?"

"About ten sections."

"Cows, too?

"No, I couldn't afford it. We'll have to grow into it."

"Jed, that's a lot of land, ten square miles. That's a lot of work. And there is Terrell to consider. I've heard some bad things about him. Probably not all true, but gossip just the same."

"Don't you worry. My brother's coming."

"I didn't know you had a brother."

"I do. James Joseph. A little over two months ago I sent him a letter. Sent it to my mother. She'll know where he is. I sent one to my sister for him. She always has a trunk full of problems. She always gets big brother to

solve them for her. She'll know where he is. Joseph will be coming. I just don't know when...but he will be here."

"Wait a minute. You have a sister?"

"Joyce Irene." he said.

"Is your brother older or younger than you?"

"Older. By two years."

"Your sister?"

"Irene. She's younger by two years."

"Jed, you've been hiding this. Does James–or is it Jim, Joseph or Joe? Does he know about your ranch?"

"Mother called him Joseph. He doesn't know. Not yet."

"You're going to surprise him? Is that wise, Jed? What if he doesn't like ranching?"

"He's my brother, Rebecca. He'll help. That's what brothers do. Besides half of it is in his name. That ought to keep him, not to mention his niece. She will seal the deal."

"Really? Did Abby agree to that?" She caught herself, feeling embarrassed by her boldness. "Not that it's my business. I'm sorry."

"No, it's all right," Jed reassured her. "No, in answer to your question. I did it after Abby passed. A year ago actually. I recorded the deeds a month after Terrell started pushing me. I thought it would be safer for me and Millie...and now, you."

"Me?"

"If I were to find myself dead, and we were married and your name was on the land, all alone, you'd be in trouble. This Terrell is crazy. Even married you'd still be in danger. That's why my brother—he's the key to peace, to Millie being safe, and to your safety. To tell the truth, the thought of Joseph being around makes me feel good, too. I'd be safe."

"Joseph can solve all of this? Sounds too good to be true. No one is that good. No one. You could be setting him up to fail. Did you ever think of that?"

"My brother? He is too good to be true. Rebecca, folks don't just kill my brother. I can tell you for a fact, he won't take kindly to it. Which brings me back to you. When are you coming home with me? I think it's time to get out of the easy chair, you and me. What do you say?"

Rebecca silently sat looking at him.

"I'll pick you up in four weeks. If it's not to be, tell me now."

"I'll be ready," she said, her heart beating in her chest as though she was a school girl holding hands for the first time. And he hadn't even kissed her. He will, she imagined.

"Good," he said.

CHAPTER 14

Jed Johnson wasn't going to be picking her up now, not anymore. Now there were just four people left: herself, Millie, Josh and Jesse. If she didn't hurry there might only be three. Rebecca Marchant wiped more tears from her cheeks. "Please God," she prayed, "please help me. I can't do this all by myself. I just can't."

What was worse, James Joseph Johnson, whoever he was, never came. Rebecca Marchant took up the slack in the reins wondering what ever happened to him. Mail was slow, she guessed. Jed sure liked his brother, but nobody was that perfect, no one that good, that reliable. Not out here. Not anywhere. She supposed that he still could come, but now it was too late. Jed was dead.

Rebecca remembered expressing her doubts several times to him about the affect that one man could have, or not have--mostly not. It was just too much to hope for she'd said to him.

Jed had laughed. "You don't know my brother." And Jed had told her a story. She expected that there were a lot of stories.

"A long time ago," Jed said, "I guess I was eighteen or nineteen, maybe. Mother had borrowed some money from some people who'd knowed my Dad. She'd made all of the payments. She told them, however, she'd be late on the last one, by one week, seven days.

"'No, you won't,' they said. 'Either pay when due or leave.'

"The next day four of them showed up in the early morning to evict Mother, claiming the house was theirs. I was asleep upstairs. Least I was until these four showed up. Their talking woke me up.

"Mother was on the front porch crying, trying to hold herself together and not doing too good of a job of it. Joseph stepped outside-- Mother always called him Joseph—we all did. He'd been eating breakfast and still had a towel covering his shirt. He liked to wear these fancy silk shirts.

"He asked Mother, 'What's the matter?' She told him, 'I asked for a week. Just a week. It's the last payment, Joseph. I only needed an extra week. I didn't think it would matter.'

"Joseph looked from my mother to the four men standing on the front lawn. He stepped down from the porch. 'My mother asked for a week,' he said to all of them.

"'So,' this dandy says, 'the note is due yesterday. Not today. Not tomorrow. And we're not giving your mother twenty-four hours, not twenty minutes, not twenty seconds. She's out and so are you. Know what I'm tellin' ya? And I mean now.'

"Joseph pulls a pistol out of nowhere, probably thin air, and shoots the man between the eyes. One second he's yapping about the awful things he's going to do to Mother and that same second he's pitching backwards. Dead.

"Now Joseph is looking at the other three, pistol in hand. He says, 'Boys, Mother asked for a week.'"

"The middle man, a skinny fellow, his watch fob hanging down low, his suit all buttoned up tight, he says, 'Son, your mother shall have a week. We're just here to make sure she knows as much. Yes, sir.'

"'Good. I don't want to see you boys here until Monday. Next Monday. Now get. And please,' he said, 'take your friend with you.' He stopped talking, paused. 'Any of the rest of you have anything to say about Monday?'"

Jed was laughing. "Believe me when I say they were shaking their heads no. On the double quick they were a-vacating Mother's front yard, carrying their dead friend between them.

"From upstairs, I could hear Joe talking to Mother. "He said, 'Mother, are you all right?'

"'Joseph,' she said, 'you killed that man.'

"'Joseph said, 'what man?' and opened the front door and went inside to finish his breakfast. When I got downstairs Mother was standing inside the front door looking at Joseph. He was at the table eating eggs and potatoes and biscuits and gravy.

"'Joseph,' she said, 'what just happened?'

"Joseph, he looks up from the breakfast table, 'Mother,' he says, 'You borrowed from some thieves. I know these gents. They break legs, arms, heads, carry young girls off from their parents, all for money, because they can, Mother, because they can. I just shot one of them dead because I can. It's the only thing they understand. You can take it to church that they won't be back until Monday. You better have the money, Mother. Do you have it? If you don't, I'll go get it.'

"'I have it. It's in the bank.'

"'Good,' he said. 'Let's pay them today.'

"We paid them that very day. I went with Mother. We even got a receipt. To this day, Rebecca, I've never seen anything like it. Mother and I walked up and knocked on the door. It opened. There was a colored fellow in a black suit holding the door open just like we were somebody. And believe me, we were nobody. It was 'Mrs. Johnson' this and 'Mrs. Johnson' that. They even offered us some tea while they counted Mother's money. I couldn't believe it. Mother got ten dollars back and they said 'Thank you.' And they said it like they meant it." He took a breath, and continued. "Things changed in our house after that."

"I imagine so," Rebecca said.

"Yes, before, Mother prayed for Joseph and me equally. Afterwards most of her praying was for Joseph."

"He sounds like a brigand."

"Now there's a big word. You mean thug, don't you?"

"Ok."

"I'll tell you this, Rebecca. Joseph is the greatest brother. There isn't anything he wouldn't do for me and I for him. I gotta tell you this. One time, Mother and I were sitting at the kitchen table, joking---playing checkers, if you want to know. There came a sharp knock at the door. I looked at Mother, she at me. We weren't expecting nobody. I got up and answered the door.

"There was a very well dressed man standing there, hat in his hand. He said to me in this very polite, deep voice. 'Is your mother at home?' Of course I said she was and invited him to step inside.

"He did so. And upon seeing Mother, he approached her, bowed slightly as if she were royalty, said, 'Mrs. Johnson, Joseph indicated that you'd be needing this money more than he.' The gent set a stack of bills on the table in front of her. On top of the bills and sideways he set another stack. That last, he said, was his gratuity payment. Then he clicked his heels together, bowed, and without a word walked out the front door closing it behind him. One thousand dollars plus a five hundred dollar gratuity payment. Out of nowhere. That happened to my mother more than once. My brother is something else."

"Is your mother still alive?"

"She is," Jed replied. "So is my sister. I'm not exactly sure about Joseph, but I just can't imagine him being dead."

"When's the last time you saw him?"

"Maybe I was twenty-three. It was before I met Abby. Oh, my," he said, "it could have been ten years ago. He never met Abby. I doubt he knows about Millie. Not unless Mother told him."

"Have you written him?"

"Yes."

"Ah, Jed. But, you can't know he's coming. You don't even know him yourself. Besides, anything could have happened to him."

Jed smiled at her, like she was the unbaptized, the unwashed, an unbeliever.

"He's my brother, Rebecca. I know it sounds crazy but it's like it's his job to make sure everything is all right in our lives: my Mother's, my little sister's. He fixes things."

Jed leaned back, enjoying the thought of all that his brother was. "I can tell you one thing. Joseph could cook. People would come from down the street just to eats his grits and greens. He was better than Mother, Irene, and me. *In my opinion, he was best at cornbread and bacon. I wouldn't throw anything he cooked out but I surely loved his cornbread and bacon--with a little butter and honey. Lordie."*

Rebecca laughed. *"This brother is quite a character."*

"You just don't know," Jed said. *"But you'll meet him. He's coming. That,"* he said, *"you can take to church."*

But he hadn't come. He wasn't here. And it was getting dark.

Darkness comes early to the forest primeval. Soon she'd drop down off of the Red Rim; she'd find the Johnson valley, thirty miles from where she'd started. The horses continued on into the night. *Keep going,* she thought. *The destination is in front of us.* She'd make it.

Rebecca Marchant was alone in the muffled silence. The road, what she could see of it, wound before her, hidden in darkness, lost in shadow. She dozed, awoke petrified, dozed again, awoke trying to get her bearings, bewildered because the horses had stopped. She wasn't moving. *God help me,* she thought seizing the brake handle. It was dark but in the starlight she could see a house, dark windows, and a door. It was closed.

CHAPTER 15

"Morning, Mr. Benjamin Terrell. What brings you out at seven o'clock with..." Sheriff McInroe glanced at the riders sitting quietly on their horses behind their boss, "twenty or thirty of your favorite gun hands?"

"You got a smart mouth, McInroe."

McInroe smiled. He knew his humor bordered on the fractious and that a good deal of the time it crossed over to ridicule. But it was morning; the coffee pot was barely steaming, and he'd just gotten to the office. He hadn't expected a full blown town meeting. But here they were, thirty or so, greeting him at the door, all sitting astride horses, some of which hadn't had the green worked out. Besides Terrell was a horse turd if there ever was one. Saying that he resembled the north end of a south bound horse put it mildly. No, straight up, Terrell was a horses' ass, plain and simple. If he didn't know better, he'd say he'd fought for the South in the great war. Come to think of it, the South would have hung him. He knew some of those boys. They'd never put up with this excuse for a bald ass mule. There was no sugarcoating this one. McInroe didn't like him.

But the Sheriff chuckled. "What can I do for you, Benny?" It was far too early to start a world war, let alone a small skirmish.

"I'm notifying you we're serving an order," Terrell declared from the top of a Roan horse.

"On me?"

"No, damn it, Bill. We'll need your help as a lawman to make it official."

Terrell leaned over and from his horse handed McInroe a coffee stained envelope. Jonesee walked up as he was reaching to receive it. McInroe turned to see who it was, recognizing him. "Jonesee. You're up a little early yourself."

"Yeah, Uncle. I got a weird feeling eating breakfast that you'd be needing me."

"Good, good. Come. It turns out I do need you. Here. Take this here paper. Read it. Tell me what it's all about."

Terrell was furious. "McInroe, that damn thing's a court order. Not meant for some snot-nosed kid. This is serious. This is court business."

"I heard you, Benny. And I'll thank you to keep a civil tongue. We're looking at it as we speak. Besides, Benny, I am drinking my first cup. I surely don't want to spill any on your Order; don't want coffee interfering with the law, especially court ordered law." He took a sip and swallowed. He sure as hell wasn't going to tell Benny he needed glasses to see to read. A blind, tottering, not to mention, older than dirt, sheriff wasn't the image he wanted to portray to Benjamin Terrell and his thirty fools at seven o'clock in the morning.

"It's a court order, Uncle."

"What does it have to say, Jonesee?"

"Well, Uncle, it says that the Johnson girl, being an orphan, is to be 'sized.'"

"That'd be 'seized,' Jonesee."

"An' protected from an unknown gunman." Jonesee paused, looked at his uncle and said, "I guess she's in some sort of danger, Uncle!"

"I see. Does it say what sorta danger, Jonesee?"

"No. That's all it says except 'It is so ordered, Rupert Dixon, Judge, Circuit Court, Red Lodge, Territory of...'"

"Got his signature?"

"Yes, looks like it."

William McInroe, whom some called Sheriff, but most called Bill, turned his pale hazel eyes to those of Benjamin Terrell, sitting above him in the middle of a nervous Roan horse. He took a sip of black coffee, no sugar, no cream, made from week old grounds and tasting a little like tar, and swallowed.

"What do you want from me?" McInroe said. The voice had a sarcastic cut to it. Impatient. The Sheriff knew Benjamin Terrell when he was just "Benny," at a time when he was just a foot soldier in "Useless Grant's" army of the Potomac, and later too, with the trail herds out of Texas to Abilene and Dodge City. He came across him again in Montana after the Custer business on the Little Big Horn. He didn't have too much good to say about him except he didn't cheat as much at cards as he used to. Of course Benny didn't play cards as much as he used to. That would explain that. Benny had to win. It was as simple as that. Everything was personal with Benny Terrell.

Now, after all that, Terrell was in the middle of the I-BAR Ranch. He'd been there for ten to twelve years. His boss had passed; Benny stayed. Maybe he was the boss. McInroe didn't know. Somehow he'd come out top dog, probably had the biggest, loudest bark. He'd hired some rowdies with someone else's money and had the biggest bite and thereafter, the most land, the greatest number of cows. Come to think of it, not long afterwards, after all this good fortune, his neighbors began falling on hard times. They died of this and that. And Benny, being the true and honorable gentleman that he wasn't, naturally helped the grieving widows by offering to buy their land, their cattle, for what he had, which often wasn't much, or so he said. After all, Benny was always going through a hard year.

McInroe took another sip from a cup that was almost empty and acted like he wasn't counting and counted. There were standing in front of him thirty-three men, thirty-three horses and thirty-three reasons not to be civil.

"What the hell are you doing, McInroe? Wasting my time?" Terrell demanded.

"Sheriff's business, Mr. Terrell. I was looking at that raven on the roof over yonder. Wondering if he was gonna rob the bank."

"You crazy son of a bitch."

"Benny, you know better than to be cursing around young folk. Especially in front of my office. Keep it up and I'll arrest you for disturbing my peace and raising hell. I'll ask you again. What do you want from me? " He wondered if he asked him the first time. Jonesee would know. He'd have to ask him later.

"I want you to duly serve that order. You're the Sheriff. It's an order."

"Let's see. You want me to serve that order. You want me to evict a seven year old girl from her home to protect her from a fellow who killed the very man you hired to kill her pa? Who, I might add, was doing a reasonably good job of 'protecting' her before he was made dead, before you all turned her into an orphan. Is that what you want?"

Benny erupted like a box of cartridges tossed into the fire box of a hot stove. "Who the hell told you that, McInroe?" His face red with wrath, he demanded, "Tell me, McInroe! I'll kill the son of a bitch before nightfall. Tell me this instant," he screeched. "Damn you! Damn you all to hell."

Terrell spun the Roan around, causing him to wheel on his hind legs, kicking dirt up on the boardwalk, jerking him so hard the gelding's mouth started to bleed.

"No, I won't," McInroe shouted back, stepping forward, closer to Benny and the edge of the boardwalk, "for that very reason. And I ain't serving that order." McInroe was surprised at himself and shocked by Ben's reaction. Hell, he'd never personally heard any of that. He'd just made it up on the spot. "Benny. Rest easy," he said. "The only man that can prove it is food for worms. He's supporting the lilac bush over at the cemetery, shot by the very man he was paid to kill. Bit of irony there, Benny. Know what irony means?"

"You SOB! If you didn't have a badge I'd kill you right now!"

"Really? And you still might, huh, Benny? If you can get away with it."

Terrell stared at him from the hurricane deck of the nervous Roan horse. "We'll finish this later, McInroe. Mark my words. This ain't over."

"Sure, Benny. Sure." McInroe wasn't altogether sure how much more he should push. But there was no backing down in Bill McInroe. There never had been. Benjamin Terrell saved him the trouble of answering that question when he nudged the Roan into motion, turning him north, trotting down the street, followed by some well paid help. *Help,* Bill thought, *that Benny might need real soon.*

McInroe was a shrewd judge of a man. He remembered the big sorrel horse, the man sitting in the saddle, the girl riding upon the shoulders, the two of them riding calmly down the street, a man who was inches from a gun battle, and knew it, who never turned right or left, never dodging what needed to be. Once or twice in his life he'd seen men like him, especially in the war. They never backed down, never quit and those folks that wanted them dead paid dearly for the funeral. Often it was their own. *Yes,* he thought, *Benny would need all the help he could get.*

The dust was settling back into the street when McInroe turned to his favorite and only nephew.

"What do you think, Jonesee? We stir them up?"

"Sure did, Uncle. Light a fire with that guy about now!"

McInroe chuckled. "Nice of you to come when you did. Did you have some of those bad, grave digging feelings?"

"No, Uncle. Just worried about you."

"Well, I wish you'd have some real bad thoughts about that bunch."

"Oh, Uncle. They are just slow."

"Slow?"

"Slow and sore."

"Jonesee, what the hell are you talking about?"

"Uncle, I don't know."

CHAPTER 16

Joe stood washing the evening dishes, listening to Millie sound out words from a small grey primer. It was an old primer, not that it mattered; cat was still C A T; dog was still D O G. And it worked. It all seemed so very familiar, a truly irksome feeling. Sometimes he wished he'd never recall anything. When he did, recollections came in a rush and left him madly confused. When all was said and done, he was no better off, not as far as he could tell. Though he still had dreams, at least he hadn't been waking up from dream upon dream lately.

Yesterday he'd dozed and found himself in a garden hoeing beets, red ones. A woman was there and she came toward him. It wasn't his mother. It wasn't the woman on the river boat. This one was different. If she'd just say her name then maybe he'd know her. Know for sure. But the woman looked away. He'd been so young. He looked in the same direction as she, and there was his brother, younger still. His brother had called him 'buzzard breath' and then he, this young Joe, returned the favor by calling his brother 'turkey brains' and 'gizzard lips.' They both ran off together with the woman laughing at them. It was so real. But it was so impossible, so strange and weird.

Tonight he wasn't dreaming. He was drying dishes when he heard something. Instantly he blew the stove lamp out, ran to the table like the hounds of hell were chasing him, blew that lamp out, seized Millie by the waist, and tried to race the darkness to the corner of the room. He didn't quite make it but he was close.

"Joe, what..."

"Shhhh, Millie. We have visitors, the kind we don't know about."

"We do?" she whispered.

"Yes. Be very still. If any shooting starts you hug the floor like it is your very best friend. Ok? Be flatter than a pancake."

"Ok," she said softly.

The sound came again minutes later. It sounded like horses, and a wagon. Joe and Millie hovered in the darkness, Joe with a pistol in one hand, and Millie in the other.

"Hello? Hello?"

A woman's voice.

"Millie, you hear that voice before?"

"Yes."

"Know whose it is?"

"Yes, Mrs. Marchant. She's Josh's mom. Mom's friend."

"Ok." Joe's mind raced, plotted, then reviewed the facts: a woman, after dark, at night, alone? Not likely, not this far from a town. Now what?

"Millie. Millie, that woman have a husband?"

"Yes."

"Wonder where he is. I haven't heard his voice."

"You won't."

"No?"

"He's dead."

"Oh. Ok. Well that'd explain his absence."

"Hello. Hello. Hello." The woman's voice was raised, frightened.

"Joe?" Millie whispered.

"Yeah?"

"She's really nice. She...Mom liked her lots. Is today a time to trust? Or is it no time to trust?"

Joe smiled in the dark. What else could he do? "Today, Millie, I believe is a time to trust. Leastwise, I hope so. You stay right here hugging the floor. I'll make sure."

"Ok," she whispered.

Rising, he walked to the front door opening it so that his left hand, holding a pistol, was concealed by the door frame. He peered out and saw a team of horses and a buckboard standing in the front yard with a woman still in the seat, two fists wrapped around the brake. Joe was prepared for something, just not a woman alone in the dark.

"Ma'am?" He said.

"Oh," Rebecca said, "you startled me!" She went on, "For awhile I didn't know what to think. I was worried. I was wondering what to do. I didn't know if anyone was here but me."

"Me, too," replied Joe. "I wasn't sure myself. If you'll wait a moment, I'll get a light."

"Thank you."

Joe lit the table lamp and the stove lamp. Next, he did the unexpected, wanting to disrupt what was. Quietly and quickly he stepped out the back door, leaving Millie waiting in the corner. Seconds later he was standing behind Rebecca's wagon, her back to him, knowing that Millie would appear in the doorway soon if he didn't hurry. As far as he could tell the woman was alone. That surprised him.

"Ma'am."

Rebecca sprang up screaming, nearly falling out of the wagon box. The horses weren't so tired anymore. They jerked forward, heads up, their ears back in anticipation, standing alertly in their harnesses ready to bolt. With the surge forward Rebecca tumbled back in the seat.

"My Lord!" she exclaimed when she was able to catch herself. "Why did you do that? I about died."

Joe stood in the shadows feeling chagrined, amazed at what he'd started by saying, "Ma'am."

Just as Joe had known she would be, Millie was standing inside the front doorway, one hand clutching the rag doll, the other on the doorframe. The lamplight behind her framed her diminutive body through the old rag of a blue dress she insisted upon wearing.

"Mrs. Marchant," she said, "Joe don't trust nobody. It keeps us alive and safe. But this was a time to trust. We just made sure it was all right."

"Oh. Ok," Rebecca replied shakily. "I'm all right with that. Really I am. I'm going to get down, if that would be good." In spite of herself she couldn't help but wonder what happened if it wasn't a time to trust. She didn't want to know, not today, not ever.

"Please do," Joe said walking around the wagon box. "Come inside. I'll see to your horses. Don't look like you'll be needing them tonight. Millie can help you if you like."

Rebecca's heart fluttered about her chest like a quick grey rabbit running from a hungry dog. She did manage to get from the buckboard seat to the ground using Joe's hand to steady herself, managed to say "yes" to something and "thank you" for something else. And Millie helped her. Later she would recall being offered something to eat. The rest was a blur.

Rebecca Marchant woke up to sunlight streaming through lace curtains and to Millie Johnson sitting on the edge of her Mother's feather mattress, watching her through round blue eyes, her blonde hair falling about her shoulders in maddening disarray. She wore a faded blue dress that had once been dark blue with rings of white flowers that formed patterns and lines. Now the dark blue had faded to light blue and the white rings had merged together, white on white, blue on blue. Once it had been long, had touched the floor, her white ankles flashing as she ran. Now skinny tanned calves hung below the hem. Once there were no patches; now there were many.

When Millie realized that her guest was awake, she smiled a seven year old smile of loose teeth, no teeth, and new teeth. To Rebecca Marchant she was absolutely dazzling, a waif to be rescued, a princess to be dressed in gowns of lace and lavender. What a wonderful way to wake up to morning.

"Good morning, Mrs. Marchant. Did you sleep well?" Millie hadn't stopped smiling.

"I did." The feather pillow she rested her head upon felt like heaven itself.

"Sweet dreams?"

"Yes, I had some. Thank you." She watched Millie bouncing on the edge of the bed. "That's a nice dress, Millie."

Millie laughed. "No, it isn't Mrs. Marchant. Joe says I ought to wear something else and let him turn this one into a dish towel with pockets. He says even that'd be a waste of time because there ain't enough threads left to dry a fork."

"He does?"

"Yeah," she said, standing and turning. "I say no. I say my Mom made this dress and my Dad patched it here and here and here and here," pointing as she spoke. "That's what I say."

"And what does Joe say to that?"

"He says I should wear 'what I damn well please.' He's funny, huh? 'What I damn well please'....whoever heard of that?" She hopped on one foot, then the other. "I've been waiting for you to wake up. Joe's making breakfast. Do you like pancakes?" Without waiting for a reply Millie rambled on, bending down to rub her toe. "Joe puts gooseberries in them. Not chokecherries. Not plums either, cause they have seeds." Standing again, and smoothing her dress, she continued. "I like them. Do you like gooseberries, Mrs. Marchant?"

"I believe I do. Yes."

"And ham. Do you like that? It's made of pig. Did you know that?"

Rebecca nodded her head that she did.

"And we have milk!" Millie whirled around in a circle, once, twice, finally coming to rest on the small dressing table stool that sat by the wall next to a dresser.

"Milk? Do you?" Rebecca was entranced. The child was so animated, so talkative, not at all like the quiet waif she remembered when Abby died.

"Yes. Joe gots a cow from up on the red ridge and she had a calf, like it was new and red and black. The calf gets two tits and we get two tits. So we have milk and stuff called butter. It's pretty good, Mrs. Marchant. Especially on hot biscuits. Do you know what bear sign is? Joe makes them sometimes when we're resting from counting cows."

"Bear sign? I don't believe..."

Millie hurried on. "Yes, and it's so good." Swinging her feet, first one then the other, she seemed to be considering something. Then she asked, "Mrs. Marchant, what are you here for? You scared us coming in the dark."

"I'm sorry."

"That's Ok. Joe really scared you, too." Millie declared.

"Yes. Yes, he did."

"Did you come to see me? Joe said you did. Mom's not here, you know. She died."

"Oh, Millie. Yes. I did come to see you. To see how you are getting along. To see if Joe would consider you living with me. That's why I'm here. Wouldn't you like that? To come live with me, Josh, and Jesse? Wouldn't that be fun for you?"

Millie looked at her and smiled brightly. "That would be fun," she said. "Josh is fun. I like Josh. He's somebody to play with. Josh is so fun." She stopped talking. "Mrs. Marchant, you're very nice."

"Thank you," she said, beaming inside. She'd accomplished the first part of her reason for coming without even getting out of bed. How about that!

"But I can't live with you, Mrs. Marchant. I live with Joe. He'd be sad if I wasn't here."

"Oh," Rebecca said. Failure so soon, and yes, she hadn't even gotten out of bed. It left her short of breath and cold. But Rebecca Marchant didn't give up that easily. She asked, "But, Millie, what do you do out here? And all alone?"

Millie stood up and walked over to the window. She pulled back the lace curtain, looking out at the morning. "Stuff. We look at cows and we count."

"Count?"

"Yes. Do you know how to count cows?"

"I....why don't you tell me."

"Well, you count their hooves and divide by four."

"Oh, I see."

Millie giggled, and turned to look at Rebecca. "But that's silly 'cause you have to lay on your belly and you could get stepped on. You can count horns and divide by two, except some don't have horns. You'll be all wrong if you do that! You know what to do? You could count tongues and divide by nothing. Or noses. Joe and me just count each one with a head. I can count to one hundred and more. Do you want to hear me?" She was off up the number chain like a squirrel collecting acorns.

Rebecca sat up, and placed her feet on the cool floor. She dressed in the midst of the number storm. Somewhere around three hundred and fifty-two, Millie led her to the kitchen. She glanced out the window. *It must be six-thirty or seven*, she thought. *Early. Too early for seven year old girls. Too early for thirty-one year old moms who'd traveled half the night.*

"How long have you been up, Millie?" she asked.

"Since o-dark thirty."

"Oh, really?"

"Yes we have to get up before the ol' red rooster."

Rebecca smiled. "Why is that?"

"Otherwise we'd have to kill him. Joe says that rooster is particularly sensitive to being killed and doesn't like talking about it much. Is that true, Mrs. Marchant? I didn't know roosters could talk."

"Well, Millie..."

Millie was off and running again, a veritable chatterbox. "Joe says the rooster can talk rooster and you have to listen really close to what he's saying. Joe says that nobody listens to him and that's why the rooster gets up so early. He wants to get the first word in."

Rebecca said "Good morning" to Joe. He smiled and offered her a chair. *Not a morning person*, she thought. He set a glass of milk by her plate and three warm pancakes. Steam was rising from them. There was butter and ham. It was easy to listen to Millie chatter about counting and a calf sucking his two tits and nothing at all. In another life she might have told her to hush. She noticed Joe seemed unbothered by her. *It was ok with him,* she thought. *Maybe it didn't matter. Maybe a child's aimless chatter was good. It certainly seemed to brighten this room.*

CHAPTER 17

The gooseberry pancakes were good. Rebecca had never had them before or made them herself. But it gave her ideas and that surprised her. There was milk and butter and the milk was cold from sitting in spring water. She dared not ask about bear sign. That didn't sound very good. But who knew? Instead she considered how to broach the subject of her visit with the gunman who, of all things, could cook more than grits and hard boiled eggs.

She didn't have to. Millie did.

"Mrs. Marchant wants me to live with her, Joe," Millie said, reaching for the milk pitcher.

Joe glanced up from an empty fork and looked at both of them without saying a word. Rebecca had imagined the conversation starting differently. She was caught unawares, unprepared, all of her thoughts suddenly fluttering around in her head like startled butterflies. For a pregnant moment that bordered on forever silence hung over the breakfast table; like whispers hidden amid the clank of knives, the rasp of forks across plates of stone. It hung until Rebecca couldn't bear it, couldn't wait to say something, something intelligent. *Just anything to fill the silence*, she thought. Both looked at her when she spoke.

"Yes," she said. "I did make the trip with Millie in mind. Her mother and I were very close. I thought that Millie being a girl, it would be better for her to be with me. She'll need a woman to..."

"I said no," Millie interrupted. "I told her we gots to count cows."

Joe smiled, nodded his head ever so slightly, reached for a pancake from the stack in the middle of the table, then surrendered his attention to Rebecca.

"Surely, surely you will see the wisdom in what I'm going to say. Millie cannot appreciate it now. She's much too young. She has no mother, no father, no family that I know of. My sons and I can be that family. She knows me. I'm no stranger to her. I can provide her with the opportunity to learn homemaking skills. I can teach her how to sew, how to cook, how to keep house, how to do laundry, how to wash clothes and mend. She'll be loved by people who love her."

To Rebecca's surprise, Joe watched her and listened and did not interrupt. Millie was trying to pour milk into a glass with varying results, yet Joe made no effort to assist her. Rebecca thought that in her "other world" she would have helped her--to prevent an accident, if for no other reason. Millie's efforts were disconcerting. She wanted to reach for the pitcher but Joe didn't move.

"She'd have the advantages," Rebecca continued, "of living in town. She could go to school with my boys. She could learn to read."

"I can read 'cat' and 'the' and 'dog' and 'cow,'" Millie said. "I'm learning."

"She could learn to write."

Millie didn't say anything to that.

"She'd be able to learn mathematics and ciphering: to add, divide, subtract and multiply."

"I can count. I can multiply by one. I can divide by one."

The glass of milk beside Joe's plate remained untouched, little beads of condensation forming on the outside of the glass, sparkling like diamonds in the sunshine streaming through the window. Millie sat quietly, the little chatterbox had disappeared; her unending supply of words had drained from her lips like melting ice. A mist formed around the edges of her eyelids, and tears had begun to well up. But the man still said nothing. He remained silent.

Rebecca was insistent. "Say something," she finally said to him. "Say anything. I... Who are you? Joe? Joe what?"

"He's just Joe," Millie mumbled, looking at her plate, her lower lip trembling ever so slightly.

"You have to have a last name. Who exactly are you?"

"He doesn't have a last name. He's just Joe." Millie was looking right at Rebecca.

"Are you going to let this child speak for you? Don't you talk? Don't you have a thought? Something to add?" She took a breath. "This is a serious problem, a very serious problem. We need to discuss this like adults. This child's life is at stake—who she is, who she will be." Rebecca's voice had risen.

Millie had gotten up from the table and was standing by Joe, her left hand resting on his knee.

"Mrs. Marchant?" she said.

Rebecca looked from Joe to her, exasperated. "Millie?" she said. "What, child? What is it?"

"I need Joe. He keeps me safe."

Rebecca sighed heavily, leaned back in her chair, and looked from Millie to Joe. She stared. "Won't you consider...?"

"No."

That was the first word this man had spoken to her the entire morning. He said "No."

"No? Not even..."

"No. Not even."

"But why? Can't you at least tell me why?"

"Ma'am," Joseph hesitated. "Ma'am," Joe continued, focusing on the woman sitting at the kitchen table. "Somewhere there's a man. I don't know him. A prankster, a trickster, perhaps. Whatever he is...he is a dealer. He's sitting at a table with a deck of cards in his hands. He shuffles them once, twice, three times. He sets them on the table. The deck is cut. He shuffles them again. He deals to you, to Millie, to me. Ma'am, Millie and I have the same cards, the exact same hand. I do not know what cards you've been dealt, but Millie and I are going to play the hand we've been dealt." Joe stopped talking, staring at her.

"That's it? What's that mean? Couldn't you ask for some different cards?" She shook her head, disbelieving. "Surely you can't reduce a child's life to a deck of silly cards. This isn't about a card game. It's about life."

"It is, Ma'am. And, yes, I could ask for another set of cards, but I can't. I won't. It just won't do any good. Ma'am, the die has been cast; the cards have been dealt; the road is before us, such as it is. We'll ride the bronc that's been saddled. We'll take what's been given us. We'll do the best that we can. That's it. There really isn't any more."

Rebecca Marchant, despite a wagonload of good intentions, despite all of her high ideals and lofty goals, goals that reached to the moon, was left speechless. What can be said to "that's it"? She realized that she was so used to having her own way that she could hardly bear losing the argument. But this time no one was listening to her.

She said aloud, maybe more to herself, to the room, to anyone who'd hear her, "They'll come anyway, you know. They'll come and take her away. They'll come with guns and horses, more horses and guns than Millie can count. And there will be nothing you, I, or Millie can do about it. Nothing." Grimly, she continued. "There will just be more trouble. Lots of trouble. And killing. Blood, and more blood. How's that for your cards?"

As though she'd thrown a switch from off to on, right to left, up to down, the man across the table changed before her eyes. She could not immediately put a finger on it. It was as if the air was sucked from the room, from her very lungs. She thought that even the lamp flickered. Of course it couldn't have, but still, she wondered.

"Who?" he commanded.

That was all he said to the statement she'd thrown into the wind. She thought about it later. What had she expected his reaction to be? Sally was right. This one was different. He didn't seem to understand what the word "impossible" meant.

"I don't know. One of my friends--her name's Sally--she said that someone was seeking a court order to get Bill McInroe to take custody of Millie."

"He won't."

"I know. I asked him. But this other one will."

"Who? You don't know who?"

"No," Rebecca hesitated. "Well, Sally said a fellow named Terrell. I don't know him. I've never met him. I don't know who he is. That's just what she said." Alarmed at his intensity, she continued. "It's just gossip. Really. I don't know what I'm saying. Somebody told somebody, who told somebody else. It may not be true. I mean, why would it be?" Rebecca paused, then continued. "She did say that the Court Order had been signed. She said that. It's so impossible. It doesn't make sense."

"You have any reason to believe that this fellow Terrell isn't already on his way to visit us right now?" The eyes were piercing. His focus was entirely on her. She could hardly move in her chair.

"No," she whispered. "No, I don't."

"But they may be?"

"Yes, they may be."

Joe sat in the kitchen chair and stared at Rebecca through unblinking, darkly hooded eyes, calculating.

"Well," he finally said, "if what you are saying is true, it would be somebody with money who wants something. We don't know what exactly. Probably the same sumbitch that killed Jed Johnson and tried to kill me. He's looking at Millie, but it isn't Millie. She's just a youngster. Me? I doubt it. I'm just in the way. He'll have to deal with me to get to Millie, to get whatever it is that he wants. That will mean gunmen, most likely. Whoever it is will know that. I'll need to find out who is calling for the fiddler to play, and who's coming to the ball to dance."

"What?" Now it was Rebecca's turn to watch him. She was baffled.

"How's your dance card, Mrs. Marchant? Full up?"

"Nobody has asked me to dance in years."

"Too bad. You are a fine looking woman. I'll be needing you to stay home from the ball. I'll need you here tonight." Rebecca was blushing in spite of herself. She didn't know why.

"All right," she replied. "I can't go anywhere anyhow. Not until morning. But..."

He cut her off. "Good. Excellent." Joe was smiling when he said those words. "Do you want anything else to eat? Otherwise, I'll clean up."

Rebecca Marchant shook her head no, though she'd eaten very little. Her appetite had disappeared with the word "no." What she saw next surprised, puzzled, and amazed her. Joseph turned his attention from her to Millie. He told Millie to stay right where she was, which was by his chair. He got his hat from the wall peg, came back and sat down beside her.

"See this, Sis?" he said. He was pointing to a gold locket on his hat band. She was nodding her head. "That's my promise to you. I'm going to take a look at who is coming to visit us. You need to stay here with Mrs. Marchant. I need you to take care of her until I return. It should be soon. Are we reading the same book?"

Rebecca Marchant could readily see that Millie was deeply affected by this man, much more than she had imagined possible. Since her father's death these two hadn't been separated. They'd eaten the same food, breathed the same air, counted the same cows, killed the same man and literally, ridden the same horse. She could see that separation was an Everest for seven year old Millie to climb. She glanced at the child. The knuckles in her right hand were white as they gripped his knee, the other was clenched in a fist. Her lower lip was trembling as she nodded her head in assent to his request. She was fighting back the tears that threatened to break away and run down her pink cheeks but she didn't give in to it. Instead, she stood straight and tall, her bare feet planted on the wooden floor. There was no give in her.

"Can you handle this?"

"You can take it to church, Joe," she said.

"I'll do that, Sis."

The preparation for Joe's leaving was made quickly. According to Abby's wind-up day clock, Joe left them standing in the doorway at 3:23 p.m. He rode out on a big sorrel with three fully loaded pistols: two in the saddle bags, one in the holster, and a rifle in the boot. It wasn't until he'd been gone for several hours that Rebecca found out that no one ever wound that clock and that everything in that household was done at 3:23 p.m.

Millie was still sitting by the window an hour after he'd left.

"Where did he get the name 'Joe'?" Rebecca asked her.

"I gave it to him."

"Did you give him that name because he looks like a Joe?"

"No."

"Have you ever seen your Uncles? Have you ever seen your dad's brother?"

"No."

"Did your dad have a picture of himself or maybe one of his brother?"

"I don't know. Maybe."

"Do you think Joe and your dad look alike?"

Millie looked up at her. "No," she said, laughing. "No. They are really different. My dad was handsome. He had my mom. Joe is just Joe."

Millie was certain, but Rebecca wasn't so sure. She'd have to look for a tintype, thinking that there most likely wouldn't be one.

Pictures were hard to come by. But, maybe, as Millie had said. Maybe.

CHAPTER 18

Joe rode hard and as fast as he could. A horse, like anyone, tires if pushed but Joe didn't know if he had any time. What was worse, he didn't know where to look, for whom he was looking, or how many. He knew that the wagon road used by Rebecca would not be used by these comers. At least he didn't think so. It was too long and there were shorter trails to consider. But he was just guessing and that aggravated him. That "guess" left two other possible routes. One was the canyon and the other was the route that he'd taken over the Red Rock Rim looking for Ed Beasley. But which one would they choose? Which one was fastest? He didn't know so he rode south over the Red Rock Rim trail for three hours then drifted east toward the canyons that he knew nothing about.

It was evening when he located them in the high canyon country--thirty-three riders, riding thirty-three horses at a trot. Judging by the looks of the horses, they'd been doing it most, if not all, of the day. They were pretty well spent and pretty close to where he didn't want them to be. The riders were spread out in a long line of horse flesh over a considerable distance, all moving northward up the canyon. The trailers couldn't see the leaders because of the twists and turns of the canyon's walls. Soon they'd be up on the Red Rock Rim. Soon they'd be looking out over the buildings of the Johnson ranch.

For an hour Joe rode the canyon rim, out of sight, keeping to the tall pine timber, knowing they were close by the racket they made. It wasn't as if they were hiding. But they did appear to be in a hurry. Their direction was certain: north. Joe waited, wondering what they would do. He'd need to slow them way down, perhaps as they came out of the canyon, wherever that was. He didn't know where it ended, but it wouldn't be far for the canyon was growing narrower with each step. Fortunately for Joe darkness comes early to a canyon, especially if it is deep, runs north-south, and is hidden in tall, ageless timber as this one was.

A halt in the cavalcade was called about six-thirty in the evening. To Joe's relief fires were built; coffee was boiled; and horses were tended to. He studied the horses as picket lines were formed. The I-BAR riders secured their horses by tying two riatas together, three times. The three lengthened ropes were then tied to the trunks of two trees over three thirty foot spans. Divided into groups of eleven, the horses were then secured to each rope and grained in rotation until all thirty-three were fed. They were far enough apart that they didn't raise a lot of hell kicking and biting at each other, perhaps too weary to cause a lot of commotion anyway. The I-BAR riders put their saddles, bedrolls, and gear along one side, and posted two guards on either end of the three extended ropes. They weren't worried, just careful. After all who in their right mind would steal horses from thirty-three, armed to the teeth, paid for killing, battle-hardened men? The canyon was only forty or so feet wide where they camped. They certainly didn't look like they expected any kind of trouble.

Hard tack and coffee, thought Joe, *that might keep them awake.* But it didn't. Within a half hour they were resting well in their bedrolls, all of them. Joe spent time finding a way to the canyon floor. It wasn't hard figuring out what to do. It was doing it. The two guards he hit over the head and dragged into the brush, tying them up and gagging them with their own bandanas. Next, he untied each line of eleven horses and led them down the canyon to the sorrel horse. At any moment he expected at least one of the thirty-three riders to jump up and start shooting. All hell would break loose. He wasn't ready for that. *There's always some nocturnal SOB that can't sleep or who won't*, he thought. But his fears were unwarranted and he soon had all thirty-three horses snubbed to his saddle horn, walking down the canyon, first at a walk, then at a trot. Two miles down the canyon he slowed to a walk and kept that pace.

Five hours and forty-five minutes later he turned the horses loose in Fred Rodger's livery stable corrals. Fifteen minutes later he knocked on the door to Fred's house, heard Fred's wife say "who's that?" and Fred grumbling something unintelligible. It was probably best it was.

Fred finally reached the front door, limping from stubbing his toe in the dark, his agitation reaching a peak of aggression seldom found in his "I want to be of help" heart. He threw open the door, mouth and hand ready to voice and demonstrate his displeasure. Joe didn't give him the chance.

"Fred. Fred, is that you?"

"Well, yes, but who the hell...?"

Joe cut him off. "Good. Remember when we first met? You asked me whether there was anything, and I mean anything--you didn't qualify it none--that you could do for me? Remember?"

"Well, I..." Fred was in that "just been woken up" stupor where thinking is impossible and talking difficult at best.

"There is something, Fred. Something that came to mind fifteen minutes ago. Maybe twenty, by now."

"What? Good Lord, man! What could that possibly be at four in the morning?" Fred had just received his first wind. "You scared the hell outta my wife. What possibly couldn't wait for a decent hour?"

"Thirty-three horses."

"What? What did you say?"

"I just put thirty-three horses in your holding pen. Your charge? What is it on a daily basis? What do you charge per day?"

"Uh. A dollar fifty, I reckon. But thirty-three head? I don't know..."

"Fred. These are three dollar a day horses. They need grain and hay. They are tired. They need to be cooled down and looked after, every one of them."

"Well, ok. Three dollars a day. But that's a lot of money. Why, that's ninety-nine dollars a day. I don't normally..."

"Yes, Fred. It is a lot of money for a lot of work. That's what you are going to charge. Understand?"

"I do. I just don't want to be taking advantage of you."

"You won't be."

"I won't?"

"No. The owner, and I don't know who that rightly is, is going to come to town about nine or ten o'clock tonight. Maybe a little sooner. He'll be footsore and plenty hot. You'll need to tell McInroe that that fellow and his men will be coming in for their horses. Ask him to help out and stick around. I don't want them to be cheating you none."

Joe turned to walk away, then reversed himself.

"Fred, I borrowed a bait of oats for ol' Dog here."

"Dog? You call your horse, Dog?"

Joe had to think about it before he answered. He didn't remember ever calling him anything at all. "Yes," he finally said. "Yes, guess I do. He's sorta confused, but he comes when I whistle and that's good. How much do I owe you?"

Fred hollered into the house. "Mary, he calls that damn horse of his, 'Dog.'" He smiled at Joe, shaking his head back and forth. "Nothing. You owe me nothing. Dog," he chuckled as he repeated it. "Comes when ya whistle. 'Confused.' I'll be damned."

"Well, thanks, Fred."

"Say. You're that feller 'Joe.'"

"I reckon I may be."

"Somebody heard that Johnson girl calling ya Joe."

Joe nodded.

"Listen," Fred hesitated, "it ain't my business."

"What ain't your business?"

"You ain't my business. But you killed that Beasley fellow and he sure as hell needed killing. Trouble is coming your way. Plenty of it. From what you're saying I'm guessing those

197

are Terrell's horses. They'd have an I-BAR on their left hip."

Joe was quiet, looking at Fred standing in his doorway in nothing but his red flannels. Brig Larson had told him a dozen times that he could learn a lot more by saying nothing than by flapping his lips just to hear himself talking.

"Folks are saying that Terrell paid Beasley, that he'd been on his payroll for some time til you come along and shoots him dead. That's just what I hear. This fellow Terrell, he's got that Napoleon thing happening with hisself. He wants more of everything. He ain't happy with what he's got. Never has been. So you be careful. That Terrell is one sour man. If those are his horses, he'll be coming to get you. Sure as hell's deep, he will."

"Terrell? That's his name?"

"More than likely."

"I have a question then, Fred. What's this Terrell want from the likes of me? You say he wants more. He doesn't even know me. Sure can't be a half-pint girl. She takes up no room at all, doesn't eat all that much, either. I have nothing! If I'm dead not a soul would know it or give a damn, except for that seven year old kid. She's depending on me to milk the cow. Can't be those buildings she calls home. They're nothing: a barn, a cabin, a set of graves and a fifteen by fifteen garden. The place don't run three hundred head. What's the fuss?

Why hire a man to kill Jed Johnson? And shoot at me? Why?"

Fred looked at him. "That's a puzzler. I don't know. It don't make no sense. He's got twenty to twenty-five sections of grass hisself. What's three more and what's three hundred head when he's got three thousand?"

"You reckon I'll have to deal with him then?"

Fred nodded, bracing himself in the door frame with one arm. "Or leave the country. Some have. Some good people, too."

"Thanks, Fred. Oh, Fred, when you get done feeding those horses, you and the Mrs. come out to the house. We'll do a little fishing. All right? First chance you get now. Bring your Mrs. and that sore toe."

"Damned if I won't."

"And damned if you do. Be seeing you soon."

Joe swung up on the sorrel and started moving north, first at a walk, then at a trot. He faded quickly and quietly into the early morning darkness, with a shovel full of stars left to guide him. *Old dog*, he thought. *What a name. Wonder if he does come when I whistle.*

Fred Rogers watched him until he disappeared from sight, then he turned, closing the door. "Mary, Mary," he said, "you hear me? Hear what I said?"

"What? Fred, why am I awake? Why are we awake?"

"Calls that damn horse of his Dog. Said he calls him Dog because he comes when he whistles. Doesn't that just take the cake? Said that horse was confused."

"Who, Sweetheart?"

"Joe."

"Joe? The Joe? That Joe? The killer, Joe?"

Mary Rodgers sat up in the dark, barely on the edge of their bed. She grabbed her face with her hands in her excitement. "Oh no, Fred. Oh no. We got to do something. That's where 'Becca went. She went to see him about that Johnson girl. I told her not to, Fred. I told her it was dangerous. What'll we do, Fred? What'll we do? We got to do something. Do you think Bill McInroe's home? My God, he better be!"

"Mary. Mary. Stop it. Stop your fretting. Don't worry."

"Don't worry? What are you talking about? She's out there, Fred. She's out there with that Joe. She's alone."

"That Joe, Mary, was standing at our doorway not five minutes ago. He just put thirty-three head of horses in the corral. They are Terrell's horses, Mary. Terrell's walking. Besides, Joe just invited me to do a little fishing. Told me to bring the Mrs."

"Walking?" Mary said. "That means all hell is going to break loose when he gets back. We better go get 'Becca anyway. We better do it right away. Don't you think so, Fred?"

"Mary, get back in bed. Hell's already out of the barn and running down the road. Rebecca is going to be all right. I'd say if she's with that Johnson girl she's about as safe as she can be. Nothing I can do would make her any safer."

"Do you think so?"

"Mary, I do. I do think so."

CHAPTER 19

About nine o'clock in the morning Fred told McInroe about the thirty-three horses standing in his corral, about the three dollars, and that Terrell and his men were on foot walking towards them even as they spoke. All thirty-three of them. Bill laughed, sat down behind his desk, and laughed some more. He got up, walked outside and looked north up Main Street, saw nothing, and came back inside and sat down. Then he laughed until his eyes teared up.

"You sure they are Terrell's horses?" he asked.

"They are his all right. I-BAR is stamped on every left hip. I guess we could take them to him, seeing how he's walking? Them being his horses an' all. He'll be plenty mad as it is."

"Hell, no. No, Fred. Let him walk. Let them all walk. Do him good. Do them all good. I don't like him. I wouldn't walk across the street to piss on him if he were on fire and burning up. Wouldn't throw him a biscuit if he were starving and my dog had just eaten a five pound steak. I'm telling you, I'd save the biscuit. Trouble will be coming soon enough. Let it come slowly."

"Ya don't like him none, huh? Probably just as well. I heard some stories lately about the trouble he's been brewing. Remember Ol' Man Truxler? He came in a couple a days ago. Had a broken arm. Had been beaten pretty bad."

"Hadn't heard that," Bill said.

"Got him over at the livery. Mary's been fixing him a little grub 'til he gets back on his feet."

"I'll have to speak with him."

Fred nodded. "Probably won't say much," he said. "He's pretty mad though. Said Terrell came to his place. Offered him to buy his place for enough cash to get outta town. Ol' Man Truxler said the offer wouldn't buy an old suit. He told Terrell to go to hell. After that Terrell's wranglers started crossing the creek and riding through his garden."

Fred paused, shifted in his chair, brought one worn boot upon his knee, and took a sip of McInroe's coffin varnish. "Well, old Truxler shoots himself a four point buck and buries it in his garden. Not too deep, mind you. He put some weights at one end of a rope and tied the other end on the buck's horns and hind end."

McInroe nodded, asked Fred if he wanted some more of his coffee. He didn't. He continued with his story.

"So, he's a sittin' in this cottonwood tree, when those boys come riding in to do their little dance in his garden. When it's just right Truxler pulls the pin on these weights. They drops from the tree and jerk that dead deer right up among those horses. Said they nearly died of fright. They commenced a bucking, throwed all three riders. Broke one's arm, snapped a cinch and they lit out like the devil himself was holding their tails and a jerking all the way. Truxler thought it was pretty funny. Said they beat the hell out of him, but it was worth it. 'Course he hasn't been back, either."

"Damn," the sheriff said, "that would have been worth seeing."

"Others' ain't so funny. Terrell told Jason Wilson--remember him?"

Bill nodded.

"Told him if he was still on his place on the morrow he'd hang every one of his picaninnies, then skin his wife. Told him right in front of his family. They just up and left. That was two, no, three weeks ago."

"Something's gotta be done, Fred. Gotta get someone willing to press charges before this is nothing but a ghost town. Gotta do something soon."

"There ain't nobody. Well, maybe ol' Joe. He don't seem to have much sense. I don't know, though. He's gotta look after that girl."

The sheriff nodded. "Yeah, he does and he will, but stealing thirty-three head of horses and putting that outfit afoot ain't going to make him a lot of friends."

Fred smiled. "No," he said, "but like Truxler said when I told him, it sure is funny. And he laughed til his arm hurt, 'til he was bawling like a baby. I didn't know what to think."

"It'll sure as hell embarrass Terrell. Everyone will know, if they don't already. Fred, I'd say the fuse is lit and burning bright. And I'll bet you ten dollars to a steak dinner that that's my nephew coming up the street and he is going to tell me he's got all sorts of bad, bad feelings."

Fred didn't take the bet because, as everyone knew, he wasn't a betting man. If he had, he'd have lost.

It was close to ten o'clock in the evening when they started dragging into the north end of town, their forty pound saddles draped over tired, aching shoulders. The boss came in with the second group. He wasn't carrying his. All were limping from blisters the size of dollars, some with bloody socks where the blisters had broken and run. Blisters for a good reason, too; they wore tall boots with spurs, with two inch underslung heels designed to keep the foot from going completely through their stirrups. It worked. It kept many a cowhand from being dragged to his untimely death. In those days every cowhand worth his salt wore them. All of Terrell's cowhands used them. They'd just walked fifteen miles over gravelly terrain in high heels, in boots absolutely not made for walking, walking done by cowhands who absolutely detested walking.

Mad, angry, pissed off, enraged, and thoroughly annoyed past reason and diplomacy, they hobbled into town. This is what the Sheriff and Fred saw as they stood in front of the livery stable doors watching the procession. Fred held a lantern in his left hand. It was so dark that if it weren't for the lantern they'd have missed them. The first of the group had already reached Main Street.

Someone spied the Sheriff and, as a group, Terrell's men turned towards the livery stable and descended on the peace officer like vultures on a buffalo cow dead for a week. Their immediate, hostile attention made the Sheriff a little nervous at first, but he soon regained his composure. Inside he took great pleasure in their discomfort, even relished it. Those Terrell gunners did look the worse for wear, and he intended to rub it in hard. Even if he had wanted to, and he didn't, he could not have helped himself.

"What seems to be the problem, boys? Nice night for a stroll."

By the time Bill had that out Benjamin Terrell was standing in front of him, his voice like ice, his anger one of barely controlled delirium. "Thirty-three horses, Bill. Somebody stole thirty-three I-BAR horses. We figure ten, twelve men came early this morning. Probably crossing Chain Canyon as we speak. Probably made the Cooley by now."

"Thirty-three horses?"

"Yes. And you'll earn your pay for sure, McInroe. We'll be hanging those sons to bitches before tomorrow night."

"How many rustlers you say?"

"We think ten or twelve. They came in the night. Had to know we were coming. The bastards. We'll be leaving at first light, McInroe. You'll need to be ready. You'll deputize all my men. This hanging will be legal. Understand?" Turning then, he spoke to the man holding the lantern. "Fred, we'll be needing your horses. We have saddles."

Sheriff McInroe hated the way Terrell took over his job, hated the very shadow he cast. "Horse stealing. That what you think, Benny?"

Suddenly, Terrell was on guard, alerted by the very way the Sheriff phrased the question.

"Yes," he said.

"Thirty-three horses?"

"Yes."

"Well, I don't know.....I think you'll find your horses over there, Benny," McInroe said, pointing. "There's thirty-three all wearing your brand. Look to be the ones you were riding yesterday, including that Roan with the sore mouth of yours."

Benny was silent. The men at his sides were looking towards the corrals, in the direction that Bill had pointed. Benny looked like he'd swallowed his tongue.

"One man, Benny. They were brought in by one man. "See if those are your horses. Take a look." McInroe stepped closer to Terrell.

"Fred here grained them twice, hayed them twice, and rubbed them down. They looked spent to the both of us. We even watered them twice. Pumped it ourselves. You'll be paying three dollars a head for that special care."

"Three dollars? Fred don't charge three dollars!" Terrell was suddenly cautious, restrained.

"He does this time, Benny. Extra care. With my help."

"That's robbery."

"What were you expecting to do to that Johnson girl when you got to the end of the Pitchfork and across the Rim? Put her on a horse? Wish her the best? Bring some flowers for her daddy's grave? You had thirty-two men for that? Or were you expecting that little girl to start shooting when you brought her all those flowers? Or was it just one man that concerned you?"

He waited. Terrell said nothing. "Three dollars, Benny."

Benny swore softly to himself, but he found a hundred dollars in his pocket, handed it to the man standing next to him who handed it to Fred. Fred went inside to get the change.

"Bill,' Terrell said slowly and in a measured tone. "I told you this wasn't over. I will deal with you and you won't be liking it much."

"How about now, Benny? Fred's not here. No witnesses except the men you've already bought and paid for."

"No, Bill. Later."

"When I least expect it, Benny?"

Fred brought the change. One dollar. He handed it to Benjamin Terrell directly. Benny folded the bill and stuck it into his pants pocket, studying the sheriff like he was some kind of piss ant he'd never seen before.

"Who was the 'good citizen'?"

"Well, Benny. It was that man you didn't hire ol' Ed Beasley to kill, the one he missed. That one mistake that bit him in the ass. Too bad I can't prove it, Benny. Too bad the only witness is dead, or you'd be hanging."

"Not likely, Bill. You haven't got the air to blow your own nose. All talk, that's you."

Benny, having said that, dismissed Bill McInroe and Fred like they were just so much chaff caught in the wind. Standing in the dull yellow lamplight they watched Benjamin Terrell chart the future of the Territory.

In the next sixty seconds Terrell arranged for the horses to be removed from Fred's corrals to those behind the Mirror hotel where it wouldn't cost him. He arranged for them to be grained double rations. He rented the entire hotel, thirty-three men to be fed thirty-three steaks with all the fixings. They watched him assign fifteen men to accompany him to the ranch and fifteen men to serve the order, bring the girl to McInroe, and kill or capture the man named Joe. He assigned two men to print up and distribute one hundred handbills that were to read:

WANTED DEAD OR ALIVE
(PREFERABLY DEAD)
JOE (LAST NAME UNKNOWN)
FOR THE MURDER OF ED BEASLEY AND
HORSE STEALING
$10,000.00 REWARD
TO BE PAID BY I-BAR LAND AND CATTLE
COMPANY
BENJAMIN TERRELL, PROPRIETOR

That was one minute's worth of talking. Fifteen seconds later Bill and Fred were left standing in front of the livery stable, Fred holding a lantern and ninety-nine dollars.

"Lord," Fred said, "can you believe that?"

"No," replied Bill McInroe, "least you got nearly a hundred dollars and we got ourselves a front row seat."

"You were awfully hard on him, Bill. You could get yourself killed, ya don't watch yourself some."

"I know. I know. It's just he's such a son of a bitch. I can't help myself. And I'm too damn old to run for cover with every wind that blows up Main Street. Trouble is I can't prove nothing. There was a time, Fred, not too long ago either, when a man didn't have to prove nothing."

Fred nodded and blew out the lantern, leaving them standing in the dark. "Wonder what's gonna happen."

"God only knows, Fred. But it don't look good for Joe."

Fred glanced at Bill. "It don't look good for none of us," he said. "Not at all."

CHAPTER 20

Joe rode uneasily for no good reason. Maybe he had the jitters because it was dark, maybe because it was too quiet. The normal sounds were there. He heard a coyote hunting, the aching sound of crickets, the dull roar of wind drifting through numberless pine needles as well as the flutter of ten million cottonwood leaves. The explosion of startled sage chickens flying from the hooves of the advancing sorrel made him jump.

There was the thought of thirty-three men walking, packing their saddles, bridles, pistols and rifles, bedrolls and coffee pots. They'd be angry, hungry and thirsty, not to mention embarrassed and footsore. But what was he to do? Let them come? They were not on a mission of mercy. He accepted the trade off-- their anger for Millie's well-being, and a few hours of relative safety. Millie's well-being? How long could that last? *Not long*, he thought.

Trouble was, they'd be back. It would not be to shake his hand, nor congratulate him on such a brilliant maneuver. They'd be back to kill him, no questions asked. Everyone west of the Blue Mountains would know they'd been set afoot, and probably what they were doing when they were relieved of those horses. Folks would be laughing. Those boys had the odds: thirty-three to one. They had to like that. They wouldn't lack for confidence, either. There would be no next time. The solution to the problem, if there was one, had to be permanent. "I wonder what that could be?" he spoke aloud. The sorrel's ears flipped back at the sound of the rider's voice.

There are three ways to reach the Johnson Valley. One: over the Red Rock Rim and across the ridge. This is the way Ed Beasley had traveled after he'd shot Jed Johnson. That was the shortest and most difficult of the three trails. Two: the wagon road which was the western most trail. It was the longest and easiest. Three: through Pitchfork Canyon. This was the quickest, yet grueling on man and beast. The latter was yet home to thirty-three men packing their earthly possession on their backs. Joe knew where they were, but not the name of the place.

Joe took the Rim, resting when he needed, moving forward as quickly as possible. He arrived in the valley past midnight, dead tired. Too tired to go inside and risk waking everyone, he chose instead to throw his bedroll in the hay loft. Three hours later he arose, saddled a bay horse, caught up his sorrel, and harnessed Rebecca's team, hitching them to the buckboard. Tolerating no lights, no fires, no talking, he woke Rebecca and Millie. They left a little before four under cover of darkness, the faint promise of a new day hanging in the East. Rebecca and Millie were in the wagon. Joe was leading the sorrel, riding the bay.

If either Rebecca or Millie had been allowed to ask why, he couldn't have told them. It was instinctive. He felt the need for their leaving. He couldn't quite articulate it. He felt they must keep moving to be safe. They had to be where they were not expected. Why? A moving shadow is difficult to track; be the shadow. Water running downhill through rocks, boulders, and gravel is hard to catch; be the water. That is what he felt. He knew that if thirty-three gun toting riders of the sage caught him it was over. Thus, he couldn't be where they expected him to be. Surprise this time was the difference in success and failure, in living and dying.

Hell's fire, he said to himself, *I don't even know where I am.*

By six o'clock the buckboard had traveled for two hours in tall timber. When they stopped for the first break and to rest the horses, Joe explained the situation to Rebecca and Millie. Telling Millie was the most difficult. *Keep it simple*, he told himself. *Go slow.*

"What's going to happen, Joe?" Millie asked.

"Don't know, Sis. We have thirty-three bad men after us. I don't see them quitting anytime soon."

"Why, Joe? What'd we do?"

"Nothing, Millie. And I don't know why. They just are."

Millie started to cry. "Where are they, Joe? Shouldn't we run really fast? As fast as we can?"

"Running generally doesn't do much good. When I left them they were walking back to town."

Rebecca looked at him, incredulous. "Walking?" she said.

"Yes. I took their horses to town after I'd popped a couple of them on the head. The rest were sleeping. Didn't put up too much fight."

"Joe, no wonder they are mad!" Rebecca exclaimed.

"Had to do it. If I hadn't they'd been sitting at our kitchen table by now eating breakfast. I could well be dead. Millie would be on her way to McInroe, if she was alive. I've no idea what they'd have done to you, a lone woman."

"Oh, my God!" Rebecca said, her hand covering her mouth, one arm wrapped around Millie, her eyes tearing up. "What will we do? Oh, Lord. What can we do?"

"Hey." His voice had turned to stone. "Get hold of yourselves. If we're going to live through this we have to have our wits about us. We cannot throw our hands in the air and scream, 'Oh God, we're going to die.' We do, we lose. We have to be ready for whatever is thrown our way. We're not dead. Not yet. I'll need your help! First thing we need to do is get the two of you into town. They will not harm you with everybody watching and the Sheriff living across the street. They may be cold hearted killers but they aren't stupid."

Joe looked from one to the other. "All right, Millie? You ready?"

"Yes, Joe, I'm ready," she whimpered, wiping the tears from her eyes with her sleeve, still crying, lips still trembling.

"I know you are, girl."

"Rebecca?"

She could only nod.

Joe studied Rebecca. He saw something familiar: being brave when bravery wasn't how she felt, smiling cheerfully when good cheer and laughter were as counterfeit as a three dollar gold piece. He wondered how she did it with life falling apart all around her like shattered glass. It was certainly something to be admired. She was in this fix all because she'd meant well. *Bad things do happen to good people.* Joe smiled. *But, maybe not this time. Maybe not at all.*

The next stop was two hours later, and so on. The day passed. Nightfall came and went. No one else was on the road; a fact that did not go unnoticed by Joe. Joe, who'd never been on the road as far as he could remember. At nine-thirty the buckboard and out rider moved slowly past the shadow of the livery stable, past Benson Street, the Old Gold Bank building, and the Mirror Hotel.

Rebecca's two room cabin was to the left, over two streets on the corner. Neither street had a name. She had no neighbors, just several lots, rotting logs, downed timber and a lot of trees. She didn't own it. No one did. She'd just moved in when she had no place to go. No one had said a word. It was simply hers, along with the corrals in the back with the three sided log shed. That's where she kept the horses and where Joe released them.

Tacked in the center of her door was a printed handbill, dark lettering barely discernable in the starlight. She pulled it from its mooring and handed it to Joe. It read:

WANTED DEAD OR ALIVE
(PREFERABLY DEAD)
JOE (LAST NAME UNKNOWN)
FOR THE MURDER OF ED BEASLEY AND
HORSE STEALING
$10,000.00 REWARD
TO BE PAID BY I-BAR LAND AND CATTLE
COMPANY

BENJAMIN TERRELL, PROPRIETOR

Rebecca had stared at the printing. Now her eyes were glued on Joe's, waiting for him to finish reading it. Millie stood between them looking up.

"Can it get any worse?" Rebecca asked.

Joe laughed, folded the handbill and stuck it in his shirt pocket.

"Why are you laughing? How can you?"

"Cause, Rebecca, things can always get worse. Often they do. You and I? We can only do what we can do. I need you to take care of this little snowflake for me. All right? I need some time to see if I can solve this problem."

In the dim light she stood there. Rebecca Marchant, a woman way past tired, way past rationality, way past coherent thought.

"Rebecca?" he said, opening the door for her. "Rebecca?" he said when she didn't move.

"Yes. Yes," she said.

Momentarily he looked at her, pausing before he knelt in front of Millie, taking the child in his arms, then holding her at arm's length just as long ago his father had held him.

"Millie," he whispered, "I need you to take care of Mrs. Marchant. I need you to help her until I get back. It is going to be hard. It's hard right now. But girl you are a Johnson. They are made out of hard. You know your job?"

"Yes," she murmured.

"I'll be back just like I promised. No excuses. You can take that to church, girl."

"Ok, Joe. I will."

With that he stood, turned and walked into the night, the shadows closing quickly behind him; a cloak of black wrapping his shoulders, and so he disappeared into the night.

Five minutes later he was knocking on Fred's door. This time Fred wasn't asleep. Mary was. Yet he was in his long flannels, trap door partially buttoned on one side. And he wasn't happy. He had to work to get the door to open.

"Fred?" Joe said.

"Gracious, Joe. Why don't you keep a decent hour? Come in, come in."

"Can't."

"Well, why not?"

"Fred, where's Terrell?"

"Well, Joe. Let's see. This morning they left with, I'd say, half of the riders goin' to that place you're staying, the Johnson place. The worst of the bunch I'd say."

"Half? Did you say half?"

"Yeah, half. The other half went with Terrell headed for the home place, south of here, I'd say twenty to twenty-five miles. Hey, Joe? Did you know he's payin' to have you kilt? Lord, Joe, ten thousand dollars!

"Ten thousand dollars, huh? I was hoping he'd offer a little more. Listen, Fred. Don't tell a soul you've seen me. Not a soul."

"All right, Joe but be careful. Do be careful. I'll not say a word. Not a word."

"Best to Mary, Fred."

And Joe was gone.

CHAPTER 21

Joe rode north into the night, then, skirting the town on the east by two miles, he turned south. Drowsiness plagued his every step. With no moon and barely a shovel full of stars to guide him, riding in thick timber that continually barred his way, he was getting nowhere. Finally on the edge of a small park, he stopped. Tomorrow would just have to wait on tomorrow. In the dim light he picketed the sorrel then listened to him crop grass. He heard a hoot owl talking, the hunting howl of a timber wolf, the scurrying of some rodent that he'd disturbed when he unsaddled. He hadn't any idea of what he was going to do. Quietly he wrapped himself in his wool blanket and, using the saddle as a pillow, laid his lanky frame down on a bed of pine needles.

Overhead the stars seemed so close that he could almost touch them. Sleep wasn't in him so he watched the stars until they were covered by drifting clouds, and pure darkness engulfed his world. He dozed thinking of aces, jacks, and pots of gold.

"You got any money, kid?" There it was plain as day. That was the hook. Both Brig and Foster had been right. After he'd been hooked they'd drag him in. Take your time they said. Look hesitant. Let them pull you in. Make them think your playin' cards is their idea.

"Me?" he said, innocently.

"Yes, I'm talking to you. Got any money?"

"Yes, Sir. I have twenty dollars. That's what I have. I've just been paid. Took me a month."

Good job, Joseph. Look stupid, look like an easy mark.

The gambler was talking to his cards, not looking at him. The player across from the gambler asked for one card; he obliged him. The skinny man that sat beside the gambler on his immediate right, folded.

"Well get over here, kid. Sit yourself down in that empty chair. We'll play some cards. This hand is about over. We need some new blood, some new money, even if it's only twenty dollars."

The gambler was still staring at his cards but the other four sitting at the table were watching Joseph. Two were grinning, their foreheads and eyes partially shaded by their hats. Even in the dimly lit room he could see greed bubbling over their collars. He imagined them thinking to themselves, "Here's a kid, a boy. Let's fleece him." The empty chair had its back to the far wall. Another day he might have waited but today the wall offered protection.

On the street side of the saloon the afternoon sunlight fell through the front door as it opened and closed. Joseph did not see that as a problem; the doorway was thirty feet away from the card table.

"Well, I don't know, sir. I don't know much about cards. I try and stay away..." Joseph paused to let himself be interrupted.

"Come on, kid. Not like we are going to tell your mother. We don't even know her." The burly man on the dealer's left laughed. "No one knows your ma, kid. Fill the chair. It's empty."

Joseph looked at the bartender and was met with a shaking head. "Don't do it. That money's too hard to come by. Think of all that coal you shoveled into that fire box."

Joseph smiled and said, "You're right. But one hand, bet a dollar, and go home. All I've lost is a dollar. On the way home, I can buy me a hat. A real nice one."

"It's your money, kid, but I wouldn't," the barkeeper said. "The only sure way to double your money is to fold it and put it back in your pocket."

Joseph laughed, nodding his head in agreement. But a dollar? He'd still have nineteen. He stopped in mid-thought and asked himself: Why are you here? What do *you want? For a second, opposing thoughts vied with each other: Take the chance out of the game of chance: Play cards: Do not gamble: Save your money: Don't do it, kid.*

"All right," he said aloud to the room, announcing his intention. "Just one hand, though. I can't be losing this money. Got to eat. Need some clothes."

"Sure, kid," the gambler said. "Just one hand. Get your feet wet. Maybe you'll win. Take forty dollars home. Easy money." He grinned at the others, knowingly. "Bet five dollars and you could win twenty-five. Ain't that right, boys?"

Joseph sat down in the empty chair, the back of his chair up against the wall. He leaned forward resting his elbows on the oak table, looking deliberately awkward. He'd been watching each of the players. The gambler had not been cheating, not that he could see, not yet. The man sitting on the right of the gambler was another story. But he could deal with that. Meanwhile he studied the cards left on the table, watching as the dealer pushed them together, then shuffled the deck. These boys had been playing all afternoon he imagined. The man on his left looked a little tired; his eyes drooped ever so slightly. The man next to him was a little drunk; his glass was empty; only a drop left in it. All the rest were stone sober. The gambler's glass was full, untouched.

"You cut," the gambler said.

Joseph cut the deck. The gambler looked at him, then at the cards, and shuffled the deck, once, twice and three times. He started dealing, moving the cards quickly, deftly across the table to the various players. Joseph glanced at the bartender polishing the glasses and setting them on the shelf behind the long bar. He thought of Foster Smith and Brigham Larson, saw them in the mirror of his mind. Foster winked at him, Brig nodded his head. Joseph smiled and remembered. "Do not gamble," they said. "Play cards. There's a difference."

For a moment he thought of them as he watched the gambler, watched him sink the hook, pull the line tight. It hadn't been that long ago. Five...no six years ago.

He had been twelve. In the hot afternoons the store was cool in the back amid the bean sacks, bolts of cloth, and cases of peach and pear tins. Foster liked to sit there when he came visiting, swapping lies, telling tales, some pretty unbelievable. He had leaned forward and set a worn deck of old playing cards on the bench in front of Joseph.

'What's that?' Joseph said. He said it like he was afraid of them. Hidden among the aces and deuces was a monster of ugly proportions. Cards were the plague or the pox or, worse, the disappointment in his mother's eyes. Foster had looked at him, casually, like he was thinking of something else. But the boy could tell Foster wasn't thinking of anything else, just him sitting on the salt block in the back of Brigham Larson's General store.

"That, my boy, is a deck of cards. Ya can't be shootin' your friends all the time. Might as well play cards."

"No. No. Mother, she....Pa, he played cards. Sir, I know it's a deck of cards."

"Matthew...your pa, he did play cards. He played cards. He did not gamble. There, boy, is the difference. I don't want you disappointin' your ma none. But think, boy. Use that head the Good Lord gave ya. Use it. Where are the folks goin' ta be that you're bent on introducin' to the next world, sendin' ta hell itself? To find those that wronged you means you're gonna have to go where they are. You're gonna have to fit in. Not stand out. Otherwise they'll see you comin' from across the big river, shoot you in the back at their first opportunity. You're gonna have ta know how to shuffle a deck of the Devil's own. We readin' the same book, boy?"

Joseph nodded, all twelve years of him squirming on the salt block, not liking what he was hearing, not wanting to hear it at all.

"Boy, there's rules, just like shootin' a pistol. You gotta know them rules in order to make the game play for you, in order to get what you want." Foster paused. It looked like he was thinking. It looked like he was considering how far to go, whether to leave it at that, or go on. He kept talking. "First: Know when to get the hell outta Dodge City. Many a cowhand didn't. If it becomes a gamble...leave. Understand?"

Foster Smith was looking directly into his eyes. The boy returned the gaze though he didn't want to. He didn't dare not look right back at him.

"You mentioned your pa played cards. I can see that his playin' makes you a bit edgy. I never seen your pa gamble. Remember that. Even when he placed a bet, he wasn't gamblin'. He took the chance out of gamblin'. You need to know what he did to take chance out of a game of chance. There are several things for you to be studyin'.

"Listen now, boy, cause I don't want to be sayin' this more than once." He took a breath, and began. "From the beginnin' of the game ya need to remember every card that's played. Every one. Second, and just as important, ya gotta know your own hand and the hand of everyone sittin' at the table, especially the fellow sittin' across from you. You'll be playin' his hand more than your own."

"You're just saying that aren't you, sir? Who could do that?"

"Boy, you know I ain't into wastin' words. Your pa, he could do it. Folks'll always tell you what's in their hand whether it's good or bad. Just watch them. If luck gives them a good hand they'll get all excited. Some will smile lookin' at their cards. They'll surely give it away. Some will scratch their chin, rub their neck, lick their lips. Maybe their eyelids will flutter more than usual; maybe they'll just look at you more than they did before, or tap a finger on the table once, twice, or tug at their beard. If you know what cards are on the table, how many has been dealt and what's in your hand, you can guess what they are lookin' at. That, my boy, is what is referred to as an educated guess. Most times that's all you'll ever have. An educated guess."

Brig Larson had been leaning back in his chair nodding in agreement, watching the boy. He chimed in.

"There is another reason for you to learn to play cards," he said slowly. "Both Foster and I have been noticin' it. Joseph, you simply ain't payin' attention. It's like you are walkin' in river fog. You're just not thinkin'. Yesterday you were shootin'. You picked where. Tell me, Joseph, where was the sun? In front of you or behind you? Which way was the wind blowin'? In your face? At your back? Where? Where were the shadows? Was the target in or out of the sun? Was it in the shadows? Where were you standin'? In shade? In shadow? In the sun? Small things, but they are the difference in bein' dead or stayin' alive. The other man will be affected by them. If he's any good at all he'll notice them even before you do."

Brig was sitting up now, leaning toward the boy. He seemed so large, so imposing. "Frankly, Joseph, you want him to deal with the sun in his eyes. You want the wind in his face so he has to blink when his eyes get dry or some dust blows up into his face. You want to be small, standin' in shadows, a mere whisper. Make the other fellow look for you. Take nothin' for chance. That's why you need to learn cards. You want to take chance out of a game of chance. You need to learn to pay attention to the details."

Foster Smith was smiling at him, his yellow teeth flashing as he spoke, "Now we readin' the same book, boy?"

"Yes, sir."

"Cut the deck."

"Yes, sir."

That wasn't the first time he'd ever played cards. It was the first time he played cards for the sake of playing. It was the first time he looked at a hand of cards and did not gamble. That afternoon he was too busy trying to figure out Foster and Larson and guess what they had in their hands. At first he lost. Time and again, he lost. But they didn't lose to him. The good ones never cheat, they admonished. That could get you killed. Just let the other folks give you their hard earned money and love doing it, and want to give you more money to get their loss back. After all, it was their money sitting on the table in front of you *begging for one more hand. That's what Foster said. That's what Brig Larson swore was the truth. Cards and guns.*

"What are you smiling about, kid? You haven't even picked up your hand."

Joseph looked at the gambler, admiring his shirt. "Sir, I was thinking how stupid I am for playing cards for a dollar when I worked so hard for the dollar. That's what I was thinking." He picked up his cards, studied them and looked up to see the dealer looking at him. A moment later, all were looking at him. "I'll take one," he said. "Just one." And he smiled.

"Hold on, kid. You have all the time in the world to lose your dollar."

But he didn't. Three hours and twenty minutes later, he was still smiling. He had two hundred forty-three dollars sitting on the table in front of him and the gambler was having to look in his wallet for more money to lose. The former card players were standing at the bar watching.

The gambler was about to deal again.

"No more," Joseph said. "It's just not your day."

"I'll say, and you are having the game of your life. How is that?"

"Luck, I guess. I never dealt one hand. I just cut the deck."

"You'll give me a chance to win some of it back?"

"Not today."

The Gambler was looking at him. "The name's Washington," he said. "And I do believe you have just fleeced the fleecer. Who taught you to play cards?"

"Foster Smith and Brigham Larson."

"They did a good job."

"Thank you."

"Since you're not going to let me win back my losses, tell me boy, what are you going to do with my money?"

Joseph smiled. "I want to buy a shirt like you have. One that feels nice on your skin. I want to get some nice clothes."

Washington nodded. "You don't buy clothes like these. You have them made." He looked at his watch. "Come with me, Boy. I'll introduce you to my tailor."

"A tailor, sir?"

"That's right. A man that makes fine clothes. The kind that you don't mind wearing. You do want the best, don't you?"

"Yes, sir," Joseph answered.

CHAPTER 22

Morning came softly. Dark rain clouds hung in the west with the unspoken promise of moisture. The smell of it was carried on cold winds that turned colder. Joe gave the sorrel a bait of oats and saw that he was rested; but it was not enough, not nearly enough. So he rubbed him down and left him grinding away at oats, his nosebag covering most of his head like a highwayman.

Unable to sit still, Joe circled the area where he'd slept; first at five hundred yards, then at a thousand. The only signs of life were four head of mule deer and a skunk. There were no recent tracks. Apparently everyone used the road. That was good. It was the ones who didn't use the road that worried Joe.

Come noon Joe moved. He saddled the sorrel but he did not ride; he walked. By the time the sun had dropped nearly to the horizon, he'd walked the better part of five miles leading his horse. The country was given to canyons so he chose one and made his way nearly to its end.

He made camp in the twilight by a seep spring. He had to rest the sorrel. Two full days of steady work wasn't good for anyone, let alone this horse who always seemed willing. Willingness was one thing; so was a big heart. But it was absolutely no good without energy and a little pop to sustain it, especially if the need was great. And the need could be great. He'd simply have to wait, though waiting wasn't what he wanted. He was no good at it. It drove him crazy.

Joe spent two days at the end of that canyon resting the sorrel, caring for it.

He heard them a long time before he saw them and cursed himself, cursed himself for staying a minute too long. What had he missed? There had been no one within miles when he left the last camp. He'd walked to save the horse. He'd taken every precaution to cover his trail. Still he could hear them. They were coming for him. Someone was a tracker. Someone surely knew what he was doing. Someone was paying attention. And that someone had found him.

Always avoid a fight. That was the silver haired woman talking, his mother. Sometimes he couldn't. And he hadn't. Why wait for what is to be? Just meet it wherever it is; introduce yourself. Get on with the living or the dying. Besides, dodging just leads to a sore neck. Running is the chief cause of busted lungs. It leaves a horse winded, short of breath, unsteady. It ruins him for life.

"Canyons? Don't be so hasty." That's what Foster Smith had said. "At their very end you'll find you can hear better. A small snap will be a big pop. It's true," he said. "Things soundin' close will be a little farther away. The canyon walls will build up your hearing. Bring sound to you. Just as important, friend or foe, they'll be comin' at you one at a time. Like a funnel. Nobody will be circlin' around behind unless they're part mountain goat. Canyons ain't bad, boy if you gotta hold up. Keep that in mind."

A twig snapped. Someone swore softly. They were maybe a hundred yards away now. They'd be climbing, and probably be afoot, trying to keep quiet. There wasn't anything quiet about brush, not unless a man was wearing moccasins and had all day. There was always the twig stepped on, the branch bent too far in passing. Unused to hiking uphill, they'd be out of breath, winded, not be as careful, not be as patient as maybe they should be.

Oh, well. Joe got out from under his blanket and pulled his boots on, but not before knocking them hard to dislodge any unwanted guests. Centipedes, scorpions, copperheads and baby rattlesnakes liked boots. He knew that as sure as he did not check he'd be damn sorry, not to mention pretty useless, and maybe even dead.

Taking his blanket in hand, he bunched it up over several rocks and a fallen tree limb until it looked just right. Last, he left his hat perched on his saddle horn, close to the bedding. It looked good. Taking his time as if he had plenty, he breathed deeply thinking there was nothing like the smell of pine in the morning, slowly he stirred the coals of yesterday's fire. He was surprised to see a wisp of smoke, and thought that coffee would be good this morning. The first rays of sunlight were touching the snow topped peaks of the far blue mountains. For a moment he looked at them then got down on his knees and blew on the coals until he had a flame, fed it some dried twigs, and settled the pot in the midst of the new fire and yesterday's coals.

A small breeze picked up. The pine needles picked up the music and began to hum, building to a roar. *They'll be here soon*, he thought and retrieved his rifle from the boot, and dug two pistols from the bottom of his saddle bags. Without thinking, he checked the cylinders, added a round in the empty chamber and let the hammer down softly. He chambered a round in the Winchester.

Morning. What an awful time to die, he thought. Certainly they could have found another time, somewhere else, for something else. Still, ten thousand dollars was powerful motivation. At forty a month and found? That was a lot of months. No wonder they were coming. It was also a lot of beans, ham and chicken eggs. Even if they shared the reward, that was half a lifetime of working for wages.

If he'd only moved on sooner. Sooner? He'd only been there two days. Besides the sorrel had been tired and he was tired. He needed the rest. If he had had some line, he'd have done some fishing. Still, if there was a next time he'd move a little sooner. There was no use borrowing trouble.

From the sound they made there were six, maybe seven men. Joe found a stack of shale rock to hide behind, then leaned up against the trunk of a quaking aspen to wait. They'd never expect that they had become the hunted, that he was waiting for them. Superiority in numbers breeds contempt and carelessness. From where he hid he could see the sorrel turn his head, his ears pointing. The coffee pot was steaming a little. The birds had stopped singing. It was as though he could feel the anxious tension of the hunters, the sweating palms, the shallow breathing. Hunting a man with a gun could do that to you. *Bastards.* It was a perfectly good morning, too.

He felt relief when he saw the first man, a mere flicker of a blue shirt lost in the backdrop of undergrowth. Joe didn't shoot. He waited.

Shaking his head, he smiled a bitter smile. This was their choice. On another day he'd have fixed them breakfast. Maybe in the fall he'd have hired one or two to gather the spring calves, to repair the barn, or get a little hay in for the winter. *Maybe*, he thought, *maybe on another day, but not this day.*

The blue shirt and another fellow wearing a dark green shirt came out to the edge of the clearing, then receded into the timber. Others were coming up behind the first two. He imagined they could see the sorrel, a slight smoke swirling up from last evening's campfire, maybe even his bedroll lying shuffled and unkempt on the ground beyond the fire. He watched the blue shirt bring his rifle to his shoulder and squeeze a shot off into the blankets from about twenty-five yards. The blankets jumped. Someone swore. Now others were running, closing in.

Joe yelled, "Over here." The shooter turned toward his voice with that "Ah shit" expression on his face. He brought his rifle around and Joe shot him through the head. Without rushing, he shot the second man, knocking him backwards into the barranca. Quietly Joe moved twenty yards along the rock outcropping before settling to wait again amid boulders and a stand of young pine trees. He didn't have to wait long.

In the stillness Joe watched a few isolated willows and cattails moving wildly. Someone was pushing them aside trying to find him. They were closing in. He didn't shoot because he couldn't see anyone to shoot, but he knew someone was there, and not just one man, either. He heard whispering for a Jake, for someone named Charley, but there was no reply. A quiet settled on the glen.

He imagined that his assailants were thinking, "What happened?" Not knowing would weigh heavily but they wouldn't back away. That was certain. It was like ten thousand dollars was sitting on the kitchen table, so close they could almost touch it, almost feel the dry crisp bills in their fingers. *Goodness*, Joe thought. *They've already got it spent.* Whiskey, women and face cards. All that cash divided eqully. And there would be more to spend now that dear Jake and dear Charley weren't answering.

The willows and cattails stopped moving. Someone was trying to outflank him. In so doing they inevitably would run into a canyon wall then into plain sight. Once they got it into their heads that they had him, they'd come all at once. He could feel them hesitate. They didn't know where he was. They still didn't know what happened to Jake and Charley. They were alone with their imagination, their fears. Maybe Jake and Charley had killed him. Maybe Jake and Charley were dead.

Joe waited, hidden in the shadows of pine, blending with grey rock like the squirrels and chipmunks. *Be patient*, he told himself.

By mid-morning they were becoming restless. There were four and now Joe knew where they hid themselves. The blackbirds who had lit and immediately flown told him, as did the chipmunk that had been chirping its warning, flipping its tail. The ground squirrel fidgeting about nothing, leaving, then coming back to fidget some more, spelled trouble. The rock dog gave two away. It seemed he didn't care much for intruders parking on his den entrance. He told the world about his displeasure with his barking. Joe didn't moved a muscle. A jaybird lit in the aspen above him, eyed him and, finding no immediate danger, flew to the camp to inspect the tepid coffee and the cold, dead, smokeless fire.

They came as he knew they would, tentatively at first, presenting small targets to draw fire. When there was none, the targets became larger, the killers bolder. One crawled out of the brush and discovered the bodies of Jake and Charley, then backed away. Soon they all knew.

The discovery made them extra careful but their patience was short and their greed growing. Carefully, they tried little diversions to flush him out, a rock thrown, a branch tossed. One brave man showed himself briefly then immediately disappeared. Silence, except for the rock dog's shrill barking, settled again over the empty camp.

There were whispers, then conversation. Their confidence increased when nothing stirred. Someone suggested that maybe Jake and Charley had killed or wounded this Joe fellow or maybe he got spooked and ran.

Thus emboldened and nudged by ever growing impatience, the first man came out of hiding. Nothing happened. He glanced at the two bodies but proceeded cautiously, expecting a trap. Joe watched his eyes dance over every nook, every cranny. After what seemed like long minutes, a second and a third ventured out into the clearing. They hung close to cover, their Winchesters shouldered, the hammers pulled all the way back, ready, waiting. The fourth was keeping himself safe. But Joe knew he was there. He could smell him, hiding, waiting, keeping out of sight. No chance, Chance. This one Joe couldn't help but like. Joe remained out of sight. They could not have seen him if they had been looking, and they were. That's when they started deriding their hidden companion for not being a man, or worse.

Joe broke cover after he heard the fourth voice walking among them.

He came to his feet, a pistol in each hand, hammers pulled far back, index fingers wrapped around the triggers. Surprised, each reacted simultaneously and yet differently to his presence. Two dove for cover while trying to shoot at a moving target, trying to be less of one themselves, and trying to get out of their own way. Two swung into action, firing before they were ready, their attempts made all the more difficult by the act of sighting down a rifle barrel with a forty-five slug slamming into their chests, shoving the air from their lungs, and the light from their eyes.

Joe walked straight at them, firing as he walked, always in the shadows, the sun at his back and in their eyes. In his mind they were like so many silver coins tossed into the air. Joe advanced, shooting before he could be shot, shooting before the coins reached their apex and started their journey down, shooting while he still could, shooting the last bottle neck from the last glass bottle, shooting to be the last man standing, just to stay alive.

And to his pleasant surprise, he was, and he did. And at the last, standing in the acrid smoke of battle, he ejected the spent cartridges, reloading each Colt, one right after the other, his heart barely beating, not a thought in his head to interrupt the flow, to cause the slightest hesitation in doing what had to be done.

Once he had reloaded, he checked each corpse to make sure it was a corpse, then he removed his tracks, the spent cartridges, and any sign of himself. Quickly, he re-saddled the sorrel, rolled his bedroll tight, and buckled it behind the cantle of his saddle. Before securing the Winchester, he replaced the two spent cartridges. All the time he was thinking that he'd been on the other side of fortunate. He knew it.

The sorrel didn't want to have anything to do with dead bodies, shying away, and acting rowdy when Joe mounted.

How he'd been found was a puzzle. He'd surely been careful. He'd stayed off the roadways. He'd moved using the creek beds and running water. He'd stayed, wherever possible, on rock and shale, using sod. He'd crossed back over his own trail. Someone had surely been a tracker, a good one. He wondered if he were among the dead.

A mile down the twisting canyon, he found six saddle horses, all with the I-BAR brand on the left hip. Swinging down, Joe unsaddled the horses, leaving the saddles stacked on the ground near a clump of sagebrush. One by one he turned them loose then remounted, following them as they moved down to the mouth of the canyon, keeping them in front of him, losing the sorrel's tracks in theirs.

Once out of the canyon, he followed the horses to the confluence of one creek with the other and then took the larger creek southward. The I-BAR horses went their way, but not far. No longer pushed they stopped to crop grass and roll on their backs. Being alone didn't seem to bother them. Joe didn't wait to watch them graze before he entered the creek and began his trek downstream, keeping to the flood waters. Several miles later he brought the sorrel out of the creek and onto sheets of quartz, granite, then shale. Later he took to the stream again and held to it for several miles before leaving the creek in favor of sod. Thus he disappeared, still wondering how the last group had found him. Good wasn't good enough, not if he was going to survive to the end of the day. Careful was going to have to be damn careful. They had found him once. They would not find him twice.

At midday he stopped, studied his back trail and dry camped. In the late afternoon he re-saddled the sorrel and doubled back, taking his time, cutting over his back trail several times just to make sure no bounty hunter was out to make himself ten thousand dollars richer. Afterwards Joe kept to the trackless back country, found another canyon, and camped off another creek in deep timber, away from pastures, cows, and anything human. He'd yet to figure out what to do.

The key was Terrell. Yet Terrell had effectively put him on the run. *No fires tonight*, he thought. *No smoke. No hunting. No boiling coffee grounds.* Terrell had thirty-two--no, less then that now--six were no longer on the payroll; he had twenty-six riders. But

Terrell might not know that, not yet. Probably the six were not missed; it would be a while.

Come evening Joe wrapped his blankets around himself and listened to the night. Sometime past midnight he drifted off to sleep. And he was glad he did. For once he was glad to find himself in another world, a world where making mistakes didn't matter because he was going to wake up in the morning.

CHAPTER 23

He was leaning against the railing, as high as he could get above the water line so as to catch the afternoon breeze coming down river. Maybe it was a real breeze or maybe it was the wind in his face as he was driven upstream by the power of steam. Behind him he could hear the thrashing of the paddle-wheel beating steadily. Below him he could see the prow cutting through the silt laden water. There was a smell about the river and a sound, not noisy but swirly and gurgly, and a deep, deep wetness. It was not a bog smell for the water was fresh, and the river, broad, and deep, nearly a mile across and always drifting toward the sea.

The paddle-wheeler was painted white but in the twilight she glowed pink. Aft, extending past the fantail across the broad expanse of water, was a long, white trail, left from the wheel beating itself against the river. Above him the stacks blew black smoke into the heavy evening air. From forward he could hear the leadsman calling out the depth. "Mark twain," the helmsman shouted before throwing the line back into the silt laden and swirling current. Only the smokestacks and the wheelhouse were higher than where he stood. He hadn't been there before, which was bad for it was really peaceful.

"What are you doing here? You're not supposed to be here." The girl's voice startled him; it took him away from the great book of the river. He turned. She was young; he guessed she was about his age, or not much older, if at all. And she was a girl; not that girls were bad or even to be avoided, but other than his sister, Irene, and his Mother, he'd had little experience with girls. And this one was well dressed, beautiful even.

Her gown fell to the deck, barely brushing the planking. She seemed to float to the railing. Her sleeves were lace to her wrists, with a cuff that dangled half way to her fingers. She wore white beads around her neck. There was a smell about her, a fragrance like lilacs and roses.

"I...," he paused, staring at her. "I'm taking a breather."

"A breather? From what?" Doubt was in her voice, distrust printed across her brow. She stared straight at him with eyes that consumed him and left him breathless.

"Shoveling coal into the fire box," he said.

"You...you work here? On this boat?"

"Twenty dollars a month. And it isn't a boat. It's a paddle wheeler. The very majesty of the Big Muddy." He smiled when he said that. In his coal blackened clothes and smudged face, he didn't feel any majesty. If he felt anything at all it was exhaustion. He'd been working for the Mississippi Steam Company for a month and some. He was tired of it. But he was strong. Shoveling coal had done that for him. Still, it was quitting time. There had to be something else, somewhere else.

"You're making fun of me," she said in a low voice, one you used sitting on the front row of church when you didn't want to be caught whispering. "I really shouldn't be here talking to you. He'll hide me when he finds out. Notice I said 'when.' That man...he knows everything. I've really got to go. Excuse me, please." She turned to leave, her skirts rustling as she moved toward the stairwell.

But he didn't want her to go. "One question," he asked to her back. "Before you go, who is this 'he' and who are you?"

She turned staring at him. "I'm Ann," she said. "And the 'he' is Mr. Packard. He owns me. Leastwise he thinks he does. He owns my parents. That's for sure. He owns this paddle wheeler gambling boat. He has rules. I can only talk to who he says I can talk to and I can only be with who he says I can be with. I don't expect a boy hired to shovel coal, with dirt all over his clothes and his face, is on that list. Now I have to go. He expects me downstairs in the ballroom, not that any dancing is done there. It's for cards."

Joseph was surprised when she said Packard. Then he thought better of the name; there had to be more than one Packard. It couldn't be the same man. That would be far too easy. Still the hair stood up on the back of his neck at the mention of that name. A rash of goose bumps ran up his backbone.

"Ma'am, one other thing, just one. Sorry to keep you, I surely do not want to be the cause of you being whipped. But can you tell me: Is that fellow, Packard, fat? Weigh maybe three hundred pounds? Given to dark clothes? Does he have a big white scar on the left side of his face? Maybe four or five inches long? Does he have a big gold watch chain? Hair black as sin, combed over his head front to back? Could that be your Mr. Packard?"

Clearly now she was alarmed with him, with his description. Her stare was intent. "Do you know him? How do you know him? Did he send you here to spy on me? You bastard! This is my place! You aren't even supposed to be here. Nobody is supposed to be here." The voice was wavering, her eyes on the verge of tears.

"Ma'am, no. I have never met your Mr. Packard. Really. I am so sorry for upsetting you. Please be on your way. I am not spying on you or anyone else. I am just here to get some air, to get away from the fire, the smoke, the heat."

"Really?"   Relief flooded her face, a beautiful face that had taken on a pinkish hue with the setting of the sun.

"Yes, ma'am, really."

She was staring at him again.   "Stop calling me, Ma'am. You couldn't be a day older than I." She paused. "I'm sorry I spoke so loudly," she said. "I thought...." She looked at him as if she didn't want to go.   "They are playing cards tonight," she said wistfully. "He's playing with a Mr. Washington. If the stakes are high enough, if Mr. Packard wins more than he loses, if he wins big, I'll be part of the stakes. Sort of a reward. So I may have to entertain Mr. Washington again. Either way I lose. It will be the third time Mr. Packard has had me entertain him.   Washington has his share of losing and then some."

"Washington a tall, dark fellow, likes to wear white clothes?"

"How is it that you work in the boiler room and know so much about the men playing cards in the card room?   Never mind.   I don't want to know. I've got to go. Last time I was late a minute he whipped me until I couldn't lie down to sleep.   Good evening." There was a finality in her 'good evening' voice.   It was a dismissal.   It was a hopeless 'We'll never meet again' voice.

Alone in the lengthening shadows, Joseph stared after her. He listened to the rustle of her skirts fade, the air still alive with her fragrance, a sight so easy to look at, even in the twilight with the paddle wheeler rolling under his heels. Foster Smith had never told him about this. Neither had Brigham Larson. He wondered why.

Upon the girl's departure and in that instant of time of being alone with his thoughts, an urge to run washed over him, leaving him cold, desperate. For a moment he was a nine year old boy again, racing, thrashing through the woods, his skinny legs thumping the earth, trying to keep up. Then anger boiled up inside him like hot, black tar as he saw his father's body lying dead on the floor of a gaming house, the fat man laughing, his watch chain jangling. There was no getting around this. Packard was someone that needed to be taken care of, someone that he had to deal with, like taking out the trash or having a Saturday evening 'Sunday go to meeting, bath. Yes, it was time to lock up the chicken coop, slop the hogs, and feed the dogs.

This day of reckoning had come much sooner than he thought it would. For months, for years, he had no idea where Packard was or even where to look for him. He'd just disappeared. In fact, Joseph had mostly forgotten about Packard. It was far more important to eat, and to give his mother some money than to search for the justice of it. Sometimes he had said to himself that it didn't matter. Except here Packard was and it did matter. He was just nineteen years old and it mattered now more than ever.

Turning, he walked slowly down the stairway across the promenade deck, then toward the boiler room. Opening the door, he felt the heat and met the glare of the black gang.

"Where you been?" Horace shouted at him. "Thought that you were goin' for a breather, not eatin' supper and gettin' drunk with the rich folks. You ain't carryin' your load, boy. And I ain't likin' that."

Joseph had to agree. He wasn't carrying his load. "Sorry," he said. "But I'm not drunk. Something came up. It was unexpected."

"I'll be bettin' somethin' came up. Geez. Did that somethin' be wearin' skirts?" No one moved. All three were staring at him, two of them caucasian and one, a negro. Joseph felt his cheeks flush at the implication of the comment.

"Sort of," he answered. "I found the man that killed my pa. He's right here on this paddle wheeler. I'm going to have to deal with this, Horace. I have no choice. I don't mean not to be working. That's not my intent."

Horace, Black Sam, and an Irishman, named Riley, were all staring at him, their faces smudged with coal dust and sweat. It was hard to read their thoughts. To these older men he was just a kid, though he didn't think of himself that way. Ever since he was ten years old he'd been working; ever since he was ten he'd been preparing for this very day, this very evening. There was no shirking it.

"What's the man be called?"

"Packard."

"Boy, that man keeps four or five strikers around him. He's never alone." Riley said, "What are you going to do? Your being dead won't make things right. You always have choices. This ain't the time to be making a bad one. You best be thinking this over."

Joseph nodded and said, "I'm just going outside, Riley. I'm just going to walk the decks and look around. He doesn't know who I am. He won't know I'm coming. He won't be worried about a kid. I doubt he knows I'm alive."

"Then you'd better clean up." Horace said. "You can't go out there lookin' like you do."

Joseph smiled and walked past the three men with whom he had worked one month and eleven days, thinking it was ironic that he had been shoveling coal for the very man that had killed his dad. He hadn't even known it. Someone else had hired him right off the docks in New Orleans. It was a company that paid his wages, board and room. And all along it was Packard.

Three steps up from the boiler room floor he was standing in the black gang's quarters. The room was neat and clean. Horace insisted on it. From under his cot, Joseph pulled his mother's trunk. She'd given it to him, said he needed it. Removing his work clothes, he poured water in the sink and rag-washed himself, top to bottom, combing his light brown hair back away from his forehead and over his ears.

At least he didn't have to shave; he was still too young to have a beard, though he did have a hair or two growing from his chin. He was not too young, however, to wear black wool pants and carry a brace of six shooters plus one. After the tails of his white silk shirt were tucked in, he strapped on his gun belt and tied the holster to his right leg. The second pistol was tucked behind his belt buckle, the third behind his belt at the middle of his back. Lastly, he slipped into a black jacket and buttoned the buttons. The clothes were loose fitting and, except for the white shirt, bordered in dark grey. There was no mirror, but he was sure he looked good. It was necessary to blend in, to look like the rest. He thought he did. He hoped he did.

The pistols weren't something he wore in public. Brig had thought it a bad idea to carry pistols until he had to. Now seemed a good time.

The last thing he did was pull each pistol from its resting place and, one by one, check the cylinders. Where there were five cartridges he filled the empty chamber, leaving the holster strap off the hammer. No time to trust, he thought. Then he walked out of the black gang cabin and into the boiler room. All three turned to look at him, staring in amazement.

'Jesus, Joseph, you're gonna get yourself killed in that get up. Are you out of your mind?" Horace said.

"I am out of my mind," Joseph replied. "I've never been in it. But, Horace, would you make sure I'm dead before you throw dirt in my face?"

Riley smiled, his teeth gleamed white against his blackened face. Black Sam shoveled coal and shook his head, keeping his thoughts to himself.

"I will. I surely will," Horace replied.

Opening the door that took him to the deck from the boiler room, Joseph stepped out into the fresh air. A tall gentleman glanced at him, a gowned woman on his arm, as if to say, "What are you doing in there?" Joseph tipped his hat to the lady.

On deck and a little self-conscious, Joseph took a breath of air and got his bearings. He noted that every man he saw was armed. A few had large, leather-sheathed knives stuck in their belts and sported ivory grips on their *pistols. Dearly he wanted to check his not so glamorous pistols again. But no. Instead he forced himself to relax and follow the crowd along the deck toward the gambling halls, staying behind and to the side of the leaders. People seemed to be coming down from the forward deck in groups. He let them pass.*

Inside he stayed close to the wall and let his eyes float over the room, seeing each table, noting who was sitting where, what they were wearing.

He found Washington and the fat man who he imagined to be Packard. Packard's arm was around the waist of the young woman he had talked to earlier. She stood motionless at his side, studying or appearing to study Packard's cards. Washington and Packard sat at the center table as far forward as possible. Joseph checked for Packard's men, someone who may be at Packard's beck and call, someone who would respond if he cried an alarm. There were a probable six, six who seemed to have nothing to do and weren't doing anything but looking around.

There had been eight when his father was killed. He wondered if they were the same, dismayed that he no longer remembered. Foster had said that everything changed over time. Indeed, it had; he didn't recognize any of them except for Packard himself.

After his initial inspection of the forward card room, Joseph explored the ballrooms and cabins forward and aft, then returned. On his left, three fiddlers were tuning their instruments, preparing to play for the evening's entertainment. Again he looked for bodyguards. Two had vanished. One was behind Mr. Packard, his arms folded. Two others were off to Packard's right side. The fourth man was playing cards at another table. Joseph crossed him off the list of problems he may have to solve.

Time to open the dance, he thought. He hesitated, and once more reviewed the room, noting again who was sitting where, the exits, and where the idlers stood. It was then that he walked up the center of the room, walked with confidence that he did not feel, walked not knowing exactly what he was going to do. Play it out, he said to himself. Be bold. Belong.

CHAPTER 24

"Mr. Washington, what a pleasant surprise," he said. "I thought it was you. And seeing you here, I thought it might be a good time to let you win your losings back." Joseph looked at the fat man. "And who might this be?" he asked.

Washington looked up from his cards.

Joseph's glance had shifted to Packard, making sure he tipped his hat to the young woman who stood at his side. She wasn't smiling. She wasn't happy and she barely looked at him. Yet, she was curious. She had not recognized him.

Washington stood up. "Pardon me. Who might you be?"

"Who might I be?" Joseph said, talking smoothly, winking. "I am sure you're not used to losing, Mr. Washington. Surely, you remember? I was that wet behind the ears kid you took under your arm and allowed to win some of your money. Two hundred forty three dollars to be exact. I do have that exact sum with me should you like to try your hand at a

game of chance. Perhaps your luck has changed for the better?"

Recognition spread across Washington's face. "You that damned kid that never looked at his cards?"

"I am that damned kid. The very one that you introduced to your tailor. I thank you. I must apologize, sir, for my manners that day. But watching you relieve those good citizens of their hard earned money, I just couldn't help myself. I just had to join in the festivities. I hope you'll forgive me for having a little fun with you."

"Indeed. I do. Please sit down. Mr Packard and I were about to play a couple of hands and perhaps take some refreshment. Oh, excuse me. Pardon my manners. Joseph," he said, "this is Mr. Packard."

Joseph had given Washington little chance of resentment, or the opportunity to say yes or no. He turned his attention to the fat man and gave Washington a moment. "Mr. Packard. The pleasure is mine. But, I'm intruding. Forgive me, I do not wish to interfere. Mr. Washington, perhaps later this evening?"

Washington wasn't letting him get away. Joseph guessed he'd been losing to Packard. "No," Washington said. "You are welcome. One more at center ring may inspire Mr. Packard to go easy on me. He's been cleaning out the old barn so to speak."

Joseph smiled graciously at Washington. "No. No," he said. "I do not want to be involved in one of those three day, no breaks, poker games. Thank you. But my promise to you, Mr. Washington, I must give you the opportunity that you asked for, to win back what I took from you. That's all. My only interest. Two hundred forty-three dollars. Certainly no match for those tidy sums you're fixing to play for this evening. A mere pittance, I'm sure. I can wait."

"No," Washington said. "Please sit down.. The big games come later this evening. Do you wish to lose it all at once, in one hand?"

"Your choice. But first, Mr Packard do you mind? A friendly wager on a single hand?"

Washington spoke up, smiling at his companion across the table. "Mr. Packard. Please indulge me and this young man."

Packard nodded his head without speaking, stroking the hip of the girl standing next to him. He hadn't said a word.

Washington allowed Joseph to cut the deck before he dealt, looking first at Mr. Packard to see if he was in. Packard nodded again. The hook, Joseph thought. Now jerk the line and jerk it hard. The cards were dealt. Joseph didn't pick up his cards. Instead he smiled at the girl and watched Packard and Washington pick up theirs before he did. His cards were back on the table face down when they looked up. Packard fidgeted in his chair.

"I'll be taking one," Joseph said. "I always like to take one. And before I do, here is my bet. Two hundred forty-three dollars." He placed the sum in the center of the table.

Washington smiled, glanced at Joseph, and also counted two hundred forty three dollars of his own and placed it on the table. "One," he said. "I'll be taking one also." Joseph noted that Washington drew his card before Packard. It should have been Packard's card next from the deck.

As Washington discarded, Packard placed his two hundred forty three dollars on the table on top of Washington's and Joseph's. Shifting his weight in his chair, he settled back, his eyes intent on studying his cards. "Two," he said. Washington dealt him two. Packard took a sip of the Bourbon that he'd been nursing, setting his glass down carefully. He threw away an eight of diamonds and a three of hearts.

Joseph took another card and threw away an ace. Washington laid his cards down slowly: two pairs: deuces and sevens and a lonely queen.

Packard laid his down: three of a kind and a pair: three sixes and two queens. He assumed he was the winner, reached and brought the pot to himself.

Joseph turned his cards over one by one: two nines, three kings. "I think I won that pot,

Mr. Packard." Joseph's words stopped him like a slap across the face.

"What?" Packard said. "What?"

"Not only did I win but I think something isn't, shall I say, proper." Joseph reached for the deck and spread the remaining cards in a fan across the table for all to see.

"Count the queens, Mr. Washington." He spoke slowly, his eyes on Packard.

Washington glanced at the cards. "Oh shit," he whispered, immediately looking up at Packard. The line was drawn tight now.

"How many?" Joseph asked.

"Two," he said. "There are two." Washington was staring at Packard, the room suddenly quiet. To put it in Foster Smith's vocabulary, "You could have heard a rat fart and it would have sounded like thunder."

Washington had risen to his feet, backing away from the table, an ugly expression on his face, his hand suddenly full of revolver. But Packard was quicker. He had pulled a sleeve gun and was firing at Washington. Two pops to the single bang of a forty-five. Washington was hit and going down. The girl standing beside Packard was screaming.

Packard had the smirk across his face of a man that had gotten his shot off first. It vanished when Washington recovered and fired again and again. Washington wasn't as badly hurt as Packard no doubt wished, especially standing in front of the business end of a colt revolver, having emptied his two shot Derringer. In that instant his body was struck by the latter's two shots. Packard's body, big as it was, fell back across the girl, shoving her to the deck beneath him. It probably saved her life; Washington was in a determined rage. From the far side of the card room three of Packard's heavies were coming to the aid of their boss. Washington, his butt on the deck and trying to get to his feet, was emptying his pistol into Packard's considerable girth.

The room exploded in a roll of thunder boxed in by four walls, mixed with screams of panic stricken women, and shouts of men trying to get at their guns. Adding to the chaos were the cries of others trying to get outside and away with nowhere to go. Joseph had backed away from the table five, then, six steps. To his left and right, men in suits and women in gowns and fashionable hats were diving for cover, no longer concerned with decorum or the pleasantries of the day.

Joseph, each fist full of pistol, hesitated, lead whistling past his ear striking the wall behind him, then commenced what one fancy dressed man later described as a Naval bombardment. The three strikers had visually latched onto Washington. Before they realized that someone else was involved, slugs were pounding their bodies, upsetting their concentration, and Joseph was looking for the fourth. He was nowhere to be found. Silence followed that storm mixed with the diminishing screams of women, the yelling of men still scrambling to get out of the way. Ten seconds had passed.

In the smoke filled room Joseph sought Packard and found him, blank eyes staring up at the ceiling. He walked forward and calmly shot him between the eyes. It was a wasted effort; he was already dead. The girl was whimpering beneath him, unable to move, her lace gown, bloody, her right arm bent back under herself, pinned. Joseph glanced about. Several of the male patrons had drawn their weapons and were staring at him.

"This man killed my father," he announced. "Packard shot him dead. Pa was unarmed, just standing beside a table. If Packard were alive, I'd kill him again."

These men who surrounded him were hardened men, pistols in hand, anger in their faces, men accustomed to weapons and using them. Some were soldiers of the late War between the States, some were frontiersmen who had made fortunes in shipping, in cattle, in buying and selling land. Death was not unknown to them, neither was what happened to cheats at cards, horse thieves, cattle rustlers and murderers. There was no sympathy in their eyes, no hesitancy in their demeanor. But they didn't book people shooting at or around their women, either. One hawkeyed gentlemen stood out from the rest, spoke, an *unwavering pistol in his hand, an inclination to use it in his stance, and an unmistakable growl in his voice.*

"You through, boy?"

"Yes, I am."

"Then help the girl."

Joseph turned to Packard a little unsure of himself. He'd been told what for by some men who knew what for. It was as though Foster Smith, Brigham Larson and his Pa were looking at him with stern disapproval. He shouldn't have shot the dead man. Not only was it a waste of lead, it could have hurt the girl. Whatever was he thinking? He could hear Foster reprimanding him. "Think, boy, think. What'd God give you that head for? Think."

Two men were pushing and pulling at Packard's body, trying to remove it from atop the girl. Packard was not cooperating. Joseph lent them a hand, grabbing a boot and pant leg. Together they managed to roll the dead man off the girl onto his back. The two turned to Ann. Joseph pulled the wallet from the dead fat man's jacket and was immediately reprimanded. Foster's words were ringing in his ears. Brig's head was shaking no. "Boy, what is important? What is not? See to the girl. You can always get coins, but ladies are damn hard to come by."

Joseph turned to her immediately, but not as immediately as Foster would have liked.

264

Ann lay on the floor sobbing, gasping for breath, her gown soaked red in Packard's blood. A man knelt on either side of her, one holding her head up and the other trying to help her get her arm from beneath her body. In the middle of this struggle, a woman arrived from nowhere, pushing Joseph and the others away. It was she who helped Ann to sit up, pulling her hair back from her face, wiping the tears from her pale cheeks. Soon three other women arrived at her side and there was no room for Joseph or anyone else. He could hear Foster laughing at him. "You should have been doin' that, boy. What were you thinkin'?"

Joseph stopped for a moment, trying to get his head about him, picked up his winnings from the table and put them in his pocket. Think, he told himself.

Behind him Washington had managed to sit up on the deck. Blood leaked from a flesh wound on his left arm and high on his thigh. He'd also been creased across the scalp. He didn't look too good with blood running past his ear and down his cheek.

"Mr Washington," Joseph said, thumbing spent cartridges from the cylinder, replacing them with new. "We even? You and I?"

The dark man looked up at him. "We are square," Washington mumbled, sitting on the floor, visibly shaken, still bleeding and needing assistance. Joseph glanced about him. No one was paying him any attention, not now.

"How you getting by?" he asked. "Can I help you?"

"I'll do."

"So I see." Joseph handed him Packard's wallet, internally glad to be rid of it. "You'll find your losings there."

"And some," Washington said, grimacing as he spoke.

"Would you do me a favor?"

"What would that be?" Washington squinted his eyes and breathed out slowly, trying to find a place on the maple decking that was more comfortable, bracing himself with his good arm. There was none to be found.

"First, may I help you up? Get you a chair?"

"Thank you. It would be appreciated."

Joseph found a chair, moved it close and helped Washington into it with considerable effort.

"So, what's the favor? What do you want?"

"When you get up and around, would you be so kind as to take a thousand of the 'and some' and take it to my mother? Packard owed her. I'm sure he'd like to make it right to her, and would if he had the chance. But your shooting put an end to that possibility."

Washington laughed, grimacing for the effort. "This wasn't about cheating?"

"For you, yes. For me, no."

"Who's your mother, kid?"

Joseph gave the gambler his mother's name, her address. Washington pulled the bills from the wallet and tossed it away with his good hand. Adroitly, he flipped through the stack of bills like he would a deck of playing cards then looked up at Joseph from the chair.

"There's a lot more here than my loss and your mother's thousand."

Joseph smiled. At least he was doing something right now. "A stake for you. And I wish you well. Now if you'll excuse me, I want to look in on this girl. I think she might need my attention. Leastwise, I hope so."

A bemused grin crossed the Gambler's face as he shook his head. "Not about cheating. Certainly about vengeance. Certainly about a boy and a girl. Be my guest, boy. There are a lot worse things. I'll see to your mother."

"Thank you, Mr. Washington. I really appreciate your kindness."

"Boy, you are most welcome. Now see to your girl."

Joseph smiled and turned, looking across the room. "Ok," he said.

"How's your arm?" He pulled a chair up in front of hers and leaned forward. Packard had bled heavily across her bosom in splatters down the left side of her satin gown. Dazed, her tresses were in disarray, some dangling *across her back, some sheltering her eyes. Her face was puffy from crying, from struggling to breathe beneath Packard's three hundred pounds of dead weight. She was not at all as composed as she had been in the evening twilight on the deck above, the upper deck where he was not supposed to be. In the smoky room, she stared at him disconcertedly. He looked at her, thinking she was as beautiful as any girl he'd ever seen.*

"I'm sorry. Who did you say you were?" She asked, blinking her reddened eyes as if she were trying to get something out of them. Tears still leaked down her colorless cheeks. Her breathing was anything but moderate, coming in erratic gasps that seemed to burst, uncontrollable, past her lips.

"I'm sorry, too," he said.

The girl hesitated. "You are?" She asked. "Why?" The acrid smoke bothered her sinuses. She sniffled, wiping her nose with her sleeve. Decorum didn't seem to matter. Her voice questioned why he was talking to her. Her eyes asked what he wanted that she did not want to give and what business did he have with her. Her tone suggested that she wanted nothing to do with him.

"Well, I shot Packard in the head when I didn't need to. I'm really sorry. You could have been injured."

"You killed him? Is he dead?" Her voice asked the question but her head and eyes

twisted, searching for Packard. She found him behind her, on the other side of an overturned chair, face up, lying on the cold decking amid poker chips and face cards. His unblinking eyes stared into the infinite space above him. Realization struck her. She gasped, her mouth dropped open, her hand covering it. For a second she was speechless.

"No," Joseph answered, "I didn't."

"You didn't?" She had turned back to him.

"He was already dead. Mr Washington killed him. I shot him afterwards. I shot him because he killed my father. I shot him because I was angry. Because I wanted to. I didn't think."

"But he's dead?"

"Yes, Ma'am. He's very dead."

"Oh my God. He is dead. He's really dead." She started to cry again, sobbing now, bending over herself as if in agony. Suddenly, she lunged across the gap that separated them, encircling him in her arms, ending up on her knees between his, crying uncontrollably, her face in his chest. Confused, Joseph was speechless. He hardly knew what to think. For one thing, he wasn't sure she knew who he was and then he thought who he was wasn't important. He hadn't told her. For another thing, he wasn't sure whether she was crying because Packard was dead or because Packard wasn't alive. Somehow, someway there was a difference and he had a difficult time figuring that out. Regardless, he was aware of this girl's arms around him, of her head against his chest. He patted her on the shoulder, assuring her that everything was going to be all right.

As abruptly as she had begun crying, she stopped and looked up at him. Pulling away, she wiped her eyes with her fingers, and her nose with her sleeve and rose to her feet. "Who are you? Am I supposed to know you?" It was if she were another person.

"We've met."

"We have?" Disbelief clouded her voice with doubt and suspicion.

"Upstairs. The upper deck. You told me I didn't belong there. Remember? You told me not to call you ma'am."

"No kidding? The boy with the dirty face?"

Joseph nodded. "Yes, the boy with the dirty face." He was a little lost now, unsure of what to do next. "Perhaps," he said. "I could get you something? Do something for you? I've already been told that I showed no proper concern for you, that I endangered your life. That I was careless."

"You've been told....By who? Who told you that?"

Joseph stood up slowly, immediately regretting having made the statement.

She was looking at him, demanding an answer. "Who?" she asked.

Dodging the question, he continued, "Could I get you out of this place? Perhaps you would like to clean up? Change your dress? I could get you a drink of water."

"Who?" She asked again. "Who told you?" Now she was insistent, asking as if it really mattered.

"Foster Smith," he replied. What else could he say? It was the truth.

"Foster Smith? Do you know him? Do you know Foster Smith?" Her voice had taken on an excited tone.

Joseph was looking at her, nodding his head. "Yes," he said. "I know him."

"He's here? What did he say? I can't believe it."

"He said," Joseph chuckled, "he said, 'Boy, what is important? What is not? Get over and see to the girl. You can always get coins but ladies are damn hard to come by.' That's what he said, if you want to know."

"You do know him. That sounds just like him. Where is he?"

Joseph hesitated knowing how crazy he sounded. "He's not here. He said it a long time ago. Sort of. He's in my head. He's everywhere I go."

The truth was what it was, and Foster Smith had said that, too.

In the confusion of a gun battle, of wounded, dead, and dying, of men looking after their women folk and women looking after their men, of overturned chairs, cards scattered to kingdom come, drinks spilled and chips flung and scattered, the girl took hold of his hands. No one had ever done that to Joseph before.

"You're that boy," she said. "You're that boy Joseph. You are Joseph."

He nodded his head. "I guess so," he said, wondering how she knew.

For a moment she kept his hands folded in hers, staring at them like they were an extension of her own. Then she looked up at him. "Joseph," she said, "would you take me home?"

CHAPTER 25

It had taken thirteen days to ride twenty miles. The sorrel was in good shape once more, having recovered from two days of extra hard use. Joe didn't like doing that to an animal. It wasn't right. Some never recovered; it broke their wind, left them useless. Combine a willing horse and a loco rider and that's what happened. The sorrel could be depended on and he couldn't do that to him again. He wouldn't do that again.

It took another three days to find the ranch buildings of Benjamin Terrell. It takes time not following roads, keeping off trails, being invisible. Once there he waited and watched from the high timber above the buildings and asked himself what to do. He could wait, shoot the man sitting on his porch while drinking his morning coffee from a mile away. That's what Terrell had done to Jedediah and to himself. But he couldn't do that.

As the day dragged on he noted that the horse traffic in and out of the ranch headquarters had begun to lessen. No one was loitering around the bunkhouse. No one was standing outside the front door, or sitting on the porch smoking cigars. In the morning there had been plenty of activity. Fourteen men had been sent north. They hadn't returned. At least their horses hadn't. Maybe the riders had. They were too far away to tell. Later, ranch hands had been sent east, ten of them. They'd come back and left again.

Joe waited another day. Last night they were there but not now. No one had returned from the north in two days. He waited another day. And began to think.

It wasn't a foolproof plan. If anything it was a fool's plan. Even Joe didn't like it, not at first. As with good plans and even good 'bad' plans, it took a while in developing. On the evening of the eighth day of dry camping in the timber above the ranch buildings, Joe lay in his bedroll and stared at the starry heavens. There were so many stars it was crazy, but there was only one North Star. It wasn't true and he knew it wasn't true but he thought that if there were no North Star no one could travel north. No one could go south, and that would be a hell of a note.

Laced in the stars were stories of Romans, Greeks, Vikings. What their relationship was he could only wonder. He couldn't find any. He knew a little about the Romans. They were the ones who paid their soldiers by the number of heads they collected. *No, maybe that was Alexander the Great.* When the Romans defeated somebody they completely destroyed the place: left not one stone on another, salted the fields so they wouldn't grow, hauled everyone left living away as slaves. *Mean bunch of bastards, those Romans.* They ruled the entire world for fifteen centuries. Joe wondered how he knew that.

The plan's implementation waited on timing. It was not Joe's intention to take on thirty riders. So he waited. There was no hurry. Lots of folks rode in and out of the home place. Five days later twelve riders showed up from the north. Over the next several days riders were disbursed in all four directions, riding in pairs mostly. There were sixteen total. He wondered if they were looking for him. But Joe didn't know and he waited. In the early mornings and late evenings he circled the ranch buildings, counted the horses standing in the paddocks, those led in and out of the barn. He noted who ate in the cook shack, who visited the main house, and who didn't. After an additional three days of watching he had a good idea of who was there and who wasn't and what they were doing.

On the fourteenth day at seven o'clock in the morning, five riders left riding southeast. Half an hour later, ten more left. They rode southwest. *Must be round up*, Joe thought. All had bedrolls tied behind their saddles, rain slickers, rifles in the boot, coats for stormy weather. A chuck wagon followed after the larger bunch. It looked like they'd be gone awhile. Nevertheless, Joe waited an hour for the fifteen riders to disappear from his sight.

Only one or two remained. Joe saddled the sorrel, checked his pistols, checked the Winchester. There were no empty chambers. There was no one to trust this morning. *Today*, he thought, *is as good a day as any to reorient the North Star.* Thus at ten-fifteen in the morning Joe mounted the sorrel, circled around to the south and rode north using the trail of the just departed cowhands to cover that of his own.

Twenty-six miles to the north Bill McInroe was heating up his morning coffee, washing his cup, and thinking about Jonesee. Rebecca Marchant was walking two boys and a seven year old girl to school, not that she needed to. Normally she wouldn't have. But Terrell's men had been around. "Where's Joe?" they asked. She didn't know. No one knew.

Three of them had been watching her house, looking at her horses. They weren't alone. Ten thousand dollars had brought a lot of strangers to town, all packing guns, waiting. *He'll be too smart to show up here*, she thought. But she'd seen crazier things. She was late. She hurried, not wanting these strangers to speak to Millie, her two sons, or her. They'd tried.

Taking his time, Joe rode past the cutting corrals, the circular horse corrals, and the larger containment facilities where they gathered the big herds in the fall. Grasshoppers fled before the sorrel's hooves as they passed long haystacks that stood on both sides of the road. With three thousand head he could see they'd need a lot of hay, and lots of horses.

The first building looming on his right was a barn: two stories of big, big barn, old, used and reused, held together by huge timbers that supported the weight of a long roof. Joe rode inside, passing stall after stall and tack rooms full of saddles, harnesses, medicine and everything from shovels to curry combs and a barrel of kerosene for lanterns. Dusty lanterns sat on shelves. Bull whips, bridles, ropes and rifle scabbards hung on the walls. By the doorway was an emery wheel and a scythe waiting to be sharpened.

Joe walked the sorrel from one end to the other then dismounted. He turned out six horses and one old Holstein milk cow from their stalls. Chickens flew out of the way as he worked. The pigeons that roosted and nested above in the rafters fluttered above him. Remounting, he removed a lantern from a hook in the alleyway, turned the wick up and lit it, watching it catch hold, burning yellow, burning bright. Replacing the chimney, he tossed the lantern behind the stalls into the dry hay. The chimney shattered on impact; lamp oil caught fire. The straw began to burn. And so it began.

The bunkhouse was next. The Terrell bunkhouse was a long rectangular building that sat back of the cook shack, between it and the barn. Joe swung down from the sorrel and left him ground hitched. Without hesitation he climbed the two steps and walked inside expecting to find a potbellied stove occupying the middle of the room, probably by the doorway. He wasn't disappointed. Three cowhands were sitting at a table playing five card stud. All three turned bare heads to him as he entered. One had a broken arm, another a broken leg. The third didn't appear to have anything broken. *Probably stove up somehow*, thought Joe.

There was no reaction from the three men. Itinerant cowhands such as Joe appeared to be were the norm and the rule. He doubted that they had ever seen him before. As of yet they weren't paying him any attention. Joe had certainly never seen them. "Howdy," Joe said. Glancing up from their cards, they nodded their heads in greeting.

Joe picked up a lamp from the closest table, struck a match and lit it, watching the wick burn bright. He threw it across the room, breaking it into pieces against the far wall. Instantly the kerosene caught fire and spread up the wall.

"What the....?" the broken-armed man exclaimed.

"Boys," Joe said, "throw your firearms." All three, even the fellow with the broken leg, were suddenly standing. He had their attention. Cards were flying; piles of matchsticks they'd used as chips tumbled to the floor. They stared for no more than an instant at him, their hustle urged on by the fire racing across the floor toward them following the running kerosene.

"We ain't carryin', Mister," the broken armed fellow said. "But what...?

"Well then, help each other out the door. As you can see, this place is on fire."

Joe didn't move. They did. Grabbing their hats, they made for the doorway, one hobbling as fast as he could, the other two helping him. "Boys," Joe said, "once outside you keep walking down past the barn. No one looks back. Otherwise, I'll have to kill you. Don't want to do that. That'd make for an unreasonably bad day."

Following them outside, Joe watched them. As slow going as they were, they didn't stop and they certainly didn't look back. Smoke poured from the open barn door. They didn't slow down to look at that, either.

Joe patted the sorrel then made his way to the cook shack. No one was inside. From the doorway he could see several long tables, chairs, a cook stove, and a large pantry.

Breakfast was over, the dishes washed and put away, and the cook must have been thinking about dinner and who would be around to eat it. A ham hung from a hook in the pantry. Some side pork was on the table, along with two sacks of flour. A large white icebox sat beside the pantry door. *I'll be damned*, he thought. *An ice box!*

It looked like the cook was expected back soon. It could have been the man he'd sent walking, the one without a broken bone, nothing wrong with him after all. He was probably just playing cards, waiting for noon, waiting to bake potatoes and fry steak. Joe, using the grip of his pistol, broke the reservoir of a lamp that sat on the closest table. The oil quickly spread. He lit it, watched it burn for a couple of seconds, then stepped outside into the late morning, late August sun. So far no alarm had been given.

Joe looked toward the main ranch house. It was a castle a hundred yards away. He could only imagine what he'd find: glass, hardwood, and brass hauled from Kansas City, Chicago, and New York, no expense spared. Joe looked up at two stories of the best that money and three thousand head of cows could buy: a sprawling roof, shake shingles, and four fireplaces, their stacks poking up into the blue sky.

Having crossed the hard packed yard, Joe climbed the twenty foot wide steps to the porch, the jingle-bobs on his spurs making music as he walked. Chairs and tables were comfortably positioned about the veranda. Someone had placed a tray of water glasses on the table by the door. Ice chunks floated in the glasses. Condensed beads had formed on the outsides. "I'll be damned," he said. Taking a glass, he drank, letting the coolness slip into his stomach, liking it. It had been a long time since he'd had ice cooled water.

Smacking his lips, he swallowed, replaced the half full glass of ice water on the tray, then moved on. The porch creaked as he opened the front door. From either side of the entry he could see fine rooms filled with memorabilia: keepsakes, collections of pistols and rifles, overstuffed chairs, tables of curiosities. His presence surprised a woman coming from the back of the house. *The kitchen*, he supposed. She stopped and looked at him. She was a young woman on the short side of thirty. A long black braid fell down her back past her waist. She had oval eyes; she was of Chinese extraction and very, very easy to look at. She reminded him of someone but he couldn't remember who. She wore a long black skirt and a black lace blouse. In her hands she held a platter of what looked and smelled like egg sandwiches.

In that awkward moment he smiled at her, touched the edge of his hat with his left hand, and bet himself that the cowhands that had ridden out that morning ate a bit differently. There were those in the big house and those who took their breakfast in the cook shack, sleeping on bunks built from rough cut timber and who, in winter, kept their hands warm around potbellied Franklins. Joe had been there.

"Ma'am," he said.

"Yes? May I help you?"

So formal. Perfect English with no accent. Well groomed. Damn, he thought.

"I'm here to see Mr. Terrell," he said easily.

"He is in there." She pointed to the room on her left, the door closed. She hesitated. "If you are not expected, he will not be happy. Perhaps you should wait until later." Joe eyed the door. "Are you expected?" she asked.

"No, Ma'am, he's not expecting me," he said. But, please," Joe said, "show me in. If you'd be so kind."

"But..." Her face, her body, her voice said to him that she thought this wasn't a good idea, that she wished he wouldn't ask, that he ought to try again tomorrow or next week, or next year.

"Please, Ma'am. I've come a long way. This won't be taking long."

Again she hesitated, finally giving in to Joe's presence. "All right," she said. "Follow me, please. But don't say that I did not warn you." She passed through the doorway, holding the sandwich tray in both hands. Joe followed. The hallway opened into another room also full of furniture. *Not a bad way to live,* Joe thought. She had gracefully entered the room, flowing into it with balance, charm, and fear.

"Mr. Terrell," she said, "you have a visitor, Sir. He said he has come a long way to see you. That it won't take long."

Joe glanced back down the hallway, saw no one.

"What?" The word was short and seemed to pop and snap like a whip. The woman, noticeably alarmed, stepped back as if to avoid being hit. Joe thought that she'd experienced this before, that this Mr. Terrell was a sleeping dog that she'd just as soon leave lie.

"You have a visitor, Sir," she repeated.

Now the man turned in the chair and saw Joe standing quietly at the edge of the room, no longer in the hallway.

"Who the hell are you?" he demanded. "What are you doing in my house?" The words came downhill as though he were speaking to a band of black sheep, or worse, a crippled mongrel begging for a crumb to fall from his table.

The woman was correct. Terrell wasn't too happy. Joe wondered if he even knew the meaning of the word.

One glance told Joe that he knew this man.

A rattler isn't hard to spot, not if a man is listening. A snake is a snake. Joe didn't take his eyes off him. Yet Joe did manage to tell the woman--no, he invited her--to move aside, to sit down, sandwiches and all. She did so.

Then Joe turned all of his attention to the now standing five foot ten inches, one hundred eighty pounds of man that was Benjamin Terrell, Proprietor, a man who obviously had not been disobeyed in a long, long time. He knew him from somewhere. But where? Something about him seemed familiar. It was the light, reddish hair.

"Wilson! Get in here." Terrell shouted.

Seconds later a much larger man, perhaps six foot two inches, two hundred and twenty pounds, appeared in a doorway to the left and behind Terrell. "Sir?" he said as he made his entrance.

"We've got ourselves an unwanted and uninvited visitor. I'd..."

"No, Wilson," Joe interrupted Terrell. "I'm invited. I've come for the ten thousand dollar reward." Joe's voice was even, unrushed, soft, yet everyone heard him clearly, even Mr. Wilson, who had advanced until he was standing slightly behind his boss and to his left.

Terrell raised his right hand. Wilson stopped.

Joe smiled. *Wilson, the lap dog. Wilson: Lay down, bark, roll over; here's your pay. Don't you dare think. You're not paid to think.*

A forty dollar a month gunman working for a plug nickel boss.

"You kill that son of a bitch?" Terrell spoke loudly, as if everyone in the room were deaf. "I want to see him myself." Clearly Terrell was in control and at the very pinnacle of his world.

And Joseph knew him.

"Suit yourself. I am that son of a bitch."

The proverbial pin could have dropped. And it did. And it was heard. Truthfully, a falling cottonwood leaf could have hit the ground and would have sounded like a clap of thunder.

The whites of Terrell's eyes seemed to grow in size. Behind him Wilson grabbed for his gun as Terrell backed up. "Kill him, Wilson. Kill him!" Terrell shouted. He reached to his left for a pistol that lay on the far arm of the overstuffed chair. Wilson had his revolver up, the hammer drawn back as Terrell picked up the pistol. A sardonic expression of glee flashed across Wilson's face.

To Joe's left the woman was screaming, dropping to the floor from her chair, her hands covering her ears and face. The room exploded into a cacophony of sound: shots fired, thunder, and the flash of lightning.

Wilson's problem, however, occurred split seconds before Terrell had backed into him and then turned to his left. Somewhere buried in that time sequence something had struck Wilson in the chest. He'd thought it was

Terrell's elbow, *the bastard.* Wilson fell backwards, grabbing his chest as his gun discharged, once on purpose, a second time as a knee jerk reaction to being hit. Blood sprayed the wall behind him as he fell, striking the floor, rolling away.

Split seconds elapsed, drawing themselves out until they seemed like days, weeks, a lifetime; then silence was sucked back into the room. Terrell had thrown himself toward the arm of the chair and over it, palming the revolver as he rolled over the chair and to his feet. He came up searching for a target. But Joe wasn't where he'd last seen him. *God in heaven,* he thought as he realized that Joe was walking right at him, both hands full of iron! Terrell got a shot off as lead streamed through his brain pan like bottle rockets. His body jumped as .45 caliber slugs destroyed heart and liver.

In those interminable seconds of time the woman, her head wrapped by her arms and fingers, huddled on the floor screaming, trying to escape the sound and the fury. Both had ended, yet she continued as though they might not be, as though it had just begun.

Standing in the pall of acrid smoke, of burnt powder, Joe waited as if he expected the dead to rise from the floor, and listened as her screaming turned to whimpers, to pleas for clemency. One pistol after another was checked; each spent round replaced. Then he turned and tapped her on the shoulder. She screamed anew, rocking back and forth, trying to escape his touch.

"Easy, lady," he said. "Easy."

Wild-eyed she stared up at him at first oblivious to the hand that reached down to assist her, then seeing his hand, grabbing it with both of hers, pleading with him in another language ostensibly for her very life.

"Easy, lady." But she was well past easy. She was well beyond recognizing a sympathetic hand or even moving from the floor's grasp.

"Just a second, then. Try and get hold of yourself. I'll be just a minute." She didn't release her grip on his hand. "Lady. Lady," he said. "I'll be just a minute."

She released her grip and her eyes followed him as he moved across the floor and rolled the body of Terrell over to look at his face. Joe shook his head in disbelief. He knew him. From the end table he picked up a lamp and smashed it against the wall, spraying lamp oil over the curtains and carpets. Striking a match, he dropped it into the lamp oil. Fire caught hold immediately. The woman started chattering hysterically in what he could only assume was Chinese. *Leastwise*, he thought, *it isn't a language I've heard before.*

Joe looked at her and smiled. He said, "Yes, I know. Crazy white folks burning a perfectly good house."

Again he extended a hand and lifted her from the floor. Together they watched the fire catch hold of the curtains and follow the lamp oil across the floor, burning the carpet, licking at the edge of the wall.

"Can you believe it? I knew that man. Been looking for him. And I found him here of all places." Grunting in satisfaction, he looked at the face of the woman standing beside him and smiled again.

"Come on, lady. Let's get the hell out of here. The place is on fire." With his hand in the middle of her back, he steered her down the hall, thinking about going back for an egg sandwich. *Eat later*, he thought.

She stood just outside the entry numbly shaking her head, way past protest, as he left her standing alone to make a short detour. She watched as he busted another lamp in the living room; struck another match; another fire started. He followed her out onto the porch, holding the door for her. Through the pane glass windows they could see the flames taking hold inside, climbing the oil soaked fabric.

"Well, lady."

She turned to his voice.

"I know you speak English. Probably better than me."

She nodded.

"Got a name?"

"Mei Ling."

"Mei Ling. A pretty name. Means beautiful bell, doesn't it?"

"You know this? How?"

"Don't ask. I really don't know. But it is a pretty name. Have yourself a glass of cold water." He handed her one from the tray and took one for himself, the one he'd started what seemed to him hours ago. She sat down on a chair, her legs giving way, yet holding the glass carefully so as not to drop it. Joe didn't seem to notice as he stared idly at the smoke and flames that were engulfing the barn. He finished the water and returned the empty glass to the tray.

"Expect it is going to be a warm one. A real nice Fall, though. Never seen the cows looking so fat and sleek." There was a moment of silence. "Ma'am, I think I'll be leaving. If I were you I wouldn't be sitting here too long. It might be getting a little warm." He lightly touched the brim of his hat. "It's been nice meeting you." The rider turned away from her, walked across the porch, stepping around a table and chairs, and started down the steps. His boots emitted the creaking, aching sound of leather on leather.

Below the wooden steps wire grass had sprouted in patches of green, light brown, and yellow. The jinglebobs chatted merrily as he walked. Across the flat, down on the other side of the barn, the man with the broken leg leaned up against the pole fence, standing with his two companions. The three watched him.

That, Joe thought, *pretty much puts an end to that.*

The sorrel turned his head toward him as Joe came into view. Out of curiosity Joe whistled. Not a real strong whistle, but good enough. The sorrel's head came up, his ears cocked forward. Joe whistled again and the sorrel started towards him, holding his head to the left so as not to step on the dragging reins. *I'll be damned*, Joe thought. He waited for the horse to come to him then grabbed the trailing reins. Joe swung up into the saddle, finding the stirrups with the toes of his boots.

Behind him smoke poured from the cook shack and the bunkhouse. Mei Ling still sat in the chair on the porch steps clutching her ice water glass in both hands. Pulling the horse around, Joe started southward, following the tracks of the outbound riders he'd watched earlier that morning. Soon, he imagined, they'd see the smoke and start back. They'd probably be riding hard. He would be long gone, his trail lost in theirs, his tracks lost in their tracks. But they'd know or suspect. Not that it would make any difference; the snake had lost its head. The good king was dead, soon to be cremated, and the North Star was reoriented. For these folks North wasn't North any more.

CHAPTER 26

Man and horse kept off traveled roads and away from trails, except the game trails made by deer, elk and moose. He kept just under the timberline, out of sight, camping in meadows with small seep springs, protected and obscured on all sides by old pine and young quaking aspen. When he could he walked the sorrel on slate rock, and in stream beds to hide his trail. He built no night fires and kept moving, finally disappearing into the deep, trackless canyons of the south country.

Below him in elevation and far to the east, down where Dryhead creek meanders until it drops into the Horn, the hornets buzzed, starting out this way and that, going and coming back, with no one to guide them. The bees were angry. The hornet's nest was burnt to the ground. They had no place to go.

To everyone's surprise Mei Ling paid them their wages and that made up for the discomfort of sleeping on the ground. They probably shouldn't have been surprised. The first of every month for the last four years she had paid each of them in cash. They didn't know it but Terrell had showed her how, showed her how much. She kept the records. She knew the payroll. And she knew where he hid the money and where he kept the key. No one else did.

Still, being paid shocked not a few. Most rode for the brand and the brand made the payroll. Some were fired. Mei Ling fired them by saying she wasn't paying them any more. The cowhands who were fired included those who wouldn't accept pay from a Chinese woman. That was particularly odd because she'd been paying them all along. Everyone who stayed accepted their regular pay for their job. This wasn't a surprise, either. They weren't being paid to shoot folks or get shot at, not any longer. The new boss, the one that made the payroll, hired an older, no-nonsense retired Army sergeant to ramrod. Under his direction it took six weeks to rebuild the bunkhouse and cook shack. The cook shack was built first; they needed a decent place to eat. Housing for Mei Ling came next; she needed a place to stay. It was more of a lean-to than housing. They waited for the bunkhouse, glad for roof and grub and a paycheck.

No one except Mei Ling knew where she got the money. All that mattered to the crew was that she continued to make the payroll and the Sergeant had something for them to do. That was important. Most assumed that, believe it or not, the Chinese woman worked for someone else who owned the ranch and had hired Terrell. Others said no. No one knew and no one asked. Joe became a fading memory because there was no one around who could pay the bounty or who wanted to. Most concluded that it wasn't right anyway. Several of the boys offered up the theory that he was dead or had gone to Texas. The prevailing story was that he'd been shot, that he rode that sorrel horse until he couldn't ride any farther and had fallen off. And somehow he'd crawled under some brush and expired along with the six missing riders.

The story of the quiet man stepping into the bunkhouse, lighting the lamp and throwing it against the wall was told and retold. In its most recent telling the three men, the only witnesses, told how he'd stepped inside, both guns blazing, shot the hell out of the place and bodily threw the three of them out into the yard, crutches, coffee pot and all. Damn near killed them, he had.

The worst thing and also the best was that the Boss Lady Mei Ling told the truth. "The gunman," she said, "walked into the house uninvited and unannounced. I told him that he ought to come back later, that Mr. Terrell didn't like unannounced guests. But he would not hear of it. Instead, he demanded the ten thousand dollar reward money for himself. Both Mr. Terrell and Mr. Wilson went for their guns. They should have paid him," she said, "because they were not nearly so good."

At round-up around the chuck wagon, drinking strong black coffee, they agreed. On a winter's evening playing cards in the new bunkhouse and eating at the new tables in Mei Ling's cook shack, they agreed. No sir, no one had ever tried to collect the reward money for their own self-capture. Never. That was one crazy son of a bitch--with all due respect and no offense intended. It was definitely owed. He'd earned it. What's a man got to do to make a dollar?

And they liked to tell how he'd burned down the main house with the Boss Lady Mei Ling sitting on a chair on the porch, him offering her a glass of cold ice water. He took one himself, talked about the weather, and how the cows looked fat that fall. That fellow had to be from Texas. No one else would do such a damn fool thing. Then they claimed him as their own because they were from Texas. They wouldn't have it any other way.

CHAPTER 27

The tall, broad shouldered man rode down from the high hill country after the first snow fell and stayed, cold and white above the timberline. He sat easily in the saddle, more a part of it than not. The sun had burned him brown except where his hat rested low on his forehead. That was unnaturally white. The light brown hair that tumbled over his collar was long, but not so long as to call undue attention to it. Fall had been a little cold at 6200 feet elevation, so he wore a sheepskin coat loosely around his shoulders. It hung to mid-thigh covering his holstered pistol with the leather strap around the hammer.

He rode in from the south side, turning neither left nor right, staying pretty much to the center of the dusty street. It was close to two-fifteen in the afternoon. Except for the horse he was riding, he looked like any other horseman passing through on a balmy Thursday. This horse, however, was a little better than most, stood a little taller, moved with a certain grace that was unmistakable.

Coming in from the south side he saw a small white church with a cedar rail hitching post on two sides; there being one in the rear where the parson lived. Next to it but set back from the road was a one room schoolhouse built close to the church so that it could be used both as a classroom and a church room, be it a Monday or a Sunday. Farther down the street on the left the Mirror Hotel sat next to the Old Gold City bank. Both of these buildings were across the street from the sheriff's office and Norm Benson's Mercantile.

All of these matters of city planning were seen by the horseman as he rode into the settlement. He'd seen it before but never coming from the south side.

Young school children were playing "kick the can" between the church and school. Out in front on the street three of the older boys were sitting on the rail fence separating street from school. They were arguing, bantering back and forth, as the horseman approached. No one remembered the man. He hadn't been seen before, so they jawed back and forth about who he was, who he wasn't, and who he might be. One claimed to have seen the horse, but it was agreed that no one knew the rider. Then no one knew the horse, either.

One ventured that it could be that Joe fellow folks talked about, that no one had seen, except maybe Fred the hostler or Josh and Jesse's mom. But they all agreed that that fellow was dead for sure, that he'd been shot and crawled off somewhere, hid himself, and died a lonely death in some hole.

The "kick the can" gang swirled around them, under the fence, to the edge of the street and back under the fence. Left in its wake was a tow-headed seven year old who also saw the horse and the rider. Only she didn't step back. She stepped forward. One step, two, three. Then she was out in the middle of the street.

The boy on the end yelled a warning. All three jumped down and tried to reach her, but they were too late the heroes. A hand reached down from the blue October sky and pulled her up, placing her deftly on the shoulders of the saddle. She leaned back, wrapping the sheepskin around herself until only her tow head and blue eyes showed. The long sorrel horse never missed a step: never stopped, never hesitated, never slowed down.

The girl snuggled against the rider, and looked up at his whiskered chin. "Where have you been?" she asked. "I've been waiting really, really long."

"Hunting. I've been hunting," he said, a rumble from deep in his chest.

"Did you get anything?"

"Just you, kid. I got you."

Millie smiled. "I'm glad you did, Joe. I was worryin'."

The sheriff, in the middle of his rocking, noted their passing. As did Fred, who was replacing old straw with new--cleaning stalls. In the middle of his labor he paused, watched the rider come and then watched him go, wondering if it was too late in the year to go fishing. He decided it wasn't. *Next week*, he thought. Next week, he'd do just that. Damned if he wouldn't.

Two boys ran across the street from the school, missed a buckboard pulled by two matched roan horses, and nearly got run over, leaving the driver pulling at reins and cursing in their wake. They turned before they reached the Sheriff's Office and ran along the edge of the rutted dirt road to a two room cabin on a corner lot that was more timber than lot.

Josh was the first through the door. "Mom! Mom!' he yelled. Jesse was right behind him, short of breath. "He's got Millie," Josh exclaimed.

"Yeah Mom, he's got Millie." Jesse echoed.

"Whoa, slow down, boys. Take it slow. Who's got Millie, Jesse? Where is she? Tell me right now!" She was staring at her two winded boys, a trace of alarm rising in her voice.

"That man," Josh said. "You know. That man, Joe. That guy that never says nothin'. That never stays nowhere. The fellow with that horse. You know."

Rebecca straightened up and walked to the door, staring out, wondering what to do. She breathed a sigh of relief, smiling to herself. Absently, she wiped her hands on a rag of a dish towel. It was hard to believe. *It shouldn't be*, she thought. Millie was going home.

The end.

ABOUT THE AUTHOR

G. R. Howe was born and raised in Northern Wyoming. He graduated from Brigham Young University with a degree in Political Science and a minor in Economics. He received his law degree from John Marshall Law School in Chicago and became licensed to practice law in 1976. He pursued a career in law for thirty years in Ventura, California. He returned to Wyoming to ranch and write western novels. He has written a collection of short stories of his hometown, Kane, a small town erased by flooding by the Yellowtail Dam Reclamation project in 1965, entitled *Short Stories Out of Kane*. *No Time To Trust* is the first of several western novels he has written.

You can visit his website, "Empty Saddles and Rusty Spurs" at www.emptysaddles.com.